Pornhibition.
By
Steven J. Richardson

To those who told me to put my humour on paper,
To the ex who said I'd never finish it,
To Nick & Simon who encourage me to carry on,
This is for you.

Prologue

"…And with this act, no longer will anyone be subject to pornographic content, neither will profit be made from sexual content regardless of how classy or graphic it is. No more will men, women, machine or animals be degraded or have to lower themselves to perform these acts. It is a new day for the United Kingdom, a clean day for the United Kingdom and a new safe world for our children to embrace." The prime minister stepped back from the microphone to ferocious cheering from onlookers, as he waved to the crowd the lakes under his armpits were visible and the sweat coming down his face resembled Niagara Falls. He had been tremendously worried about how his speech would go down; opinion polls divided the public fifty-fifty in the lead up to the vote. Speculation led to believe that if people who opposed the ban on pornography used their writing hand to fill out a voting slip instead of using it to click on one last pornographic video then the vote could have gone the other way. Alas, sixty-five per cent of voters decided to agree with a ban on all pornographic content, starting immediately.

Following the announcement, those surrounding the media had differing opinions. TV news shows applauded it, and not surprisingly, broadcasted many an interview from people in the general public reacting positively to the news, panel shows wasted no time in using it for new material and people laughed and groaned at the low calibre comedy which consisted mainly of masturbation jokes. Broadsheet newspapers also took the chance to put a positive spin on the story proclaiming the change can only be positive and that children will be growing up with newfound innocence again, sexually transmitted diseases would be on the decline as well as teenage pregnancies. Some of the newspapers were receptive, others spun stories of worry suggesting it would see an increase in sex trafficking and prostitution. One paper claimed terrorists set up the whole thing and the red top tabloids took their biggest sales decline since they were told to remove breasts from page three a few years prior, they also now had to wait and wonder what kind of letters would be sent in to the agony aunts now nothing explicit could be printed.

True enough many supported the new law, not just those in attendance applauding at the prime minister's conference, but up and down the country the news was well received. The older generation, pensioners, were very vocal in their support. In a poll on people aged sixty-five or over a whopping eighty-three percent agreed with the act to prohibit pornography however another poll four months prior revealed that seventy-two percent of people aged in the same bracket did not truly know how to use the internet, they were already sheltered. Parents, giving complete disregard that watching adult entertainment led to many a child being accidentally conceived, were another keen supporter of the cause, relieved that they can bring up their children in a world without exposure to explicit content. A lower risk of catching disease and a decrease of teenage pregnancies were the positives they were hoping to see. Them aside, support came from other avenues; including religious types, politicians and those working in education. A high number of celebrities spoke out, however hypocritical they sounded, including a certain blonde-haired, busty, belly dancing popstar whose number one hit of the year included the lyrics "It's rude not to touch a dude" and many other people not wanting to look politically incorrect in the public limelight.

Then there were the critics. It had been labelled in some social circles as a dark day and that many people at work, bars, wherever they may have been when the news broke may as well have been in the country's largest communal library as they fell into a synchronized silence. All sorts of men; straight, gay and the freaky people that searched for content others would not even think of mourned their loss, it was not uncommon to see men wearing black armbands to work the first week after the vote passed. Even a large array of women hated the new restrictions on erotic entertainment, including those who were stunned to find some of their short escapist novels were deemed explicit enough to be banned. These people made last minute deposits into their wank banks, hoping to store memories before it was taken from them. First there was the nationwide media burning, Magazines, DVD's, the ancient playback devices known as VHS's, newspapers and more were put into heaps and set alight, there were cheers, there were tears, it was as if Guy Fawkes personally goose-stepped to each mound setting set them on fire. Minor riots broke out, as police had to fight back married men from trying to jump onto the flames to retrieve their valued good's. One man doused himself in petrol and threatened to set himself on fire unless he got his stash back; thankfully, he was talked out of it and made to see sense.

"What was I thinking." he was heard to say as he walked away chuckling to himself, sadly to calm down he decided to light up a cigarette.

Some people even fled abroad where they could no longer be oppressed, America, France and Italy were popular destinations for the regular porn connoisseur, Germany was the target for fans of more extreme fetishes and for those who preferred more cultural pornography, South America and Asia was frequented. Then came the deletion of all the digital media, Internet blocks were put in place, a new webcam was implemented into every home to detect and shut down if nudity was detected and lastly hard drives were wiped, it was a tough task but in due course every home was clear of pornography.

Two weeks later the prime minister was at number ten still in denial with a sense of feeling that he made the wrong decision pushing for the prohibition and authorising vote. He felt he had betrayed his country and furthermore betrayed himself. At this moment in time though he was one of the lucky ones, the internet blocks were in place two days after the law came into place and the media burning was completed in the first week but the wiping of all hard drives, whilst being praised for creating jobs which may secure a couple of votes next election, was still ongoing. Naturally, the nation's leader had arranged for his to be one of the last to be erased. These past two weeks had been all about making the most of his alone time and once more he sat at his office chair; loosened his belt, unzipped his trousers, opened his laptop and clicked on the one folder no prime minister clicks 'Lower taxes'. This was where his pornographic sanctuary was hidden, eight gigabytes of videos and pictures laid in wait for when he needed to unload stress. The folder was empty. He decided not to worry, all good prime ministers had contingency plans, and his was in the shape of his busty secretary who was always on offer to lend a helping hand. As he pressed the button on the intercom, a male's voice answered. His heart erupted like a volcano. He had forgotten his usual secretary had been signed off work sick for four months. Panic had now set it. He scrambled around on his desk before picking up a framed photograph of his wife, a tear rolled down his cheek as he stroked the picture of his significant other. He placed the photo down, reached inside his desk, pulled out a revolver, and pressed the cold gun firmly against his temple, glancing at his wife one last time he closed his eyes tightly and squeezed the finger resting on the trigger.

ONE YEAR LATER and the embargo is in full effect.

CHAPTER 1

It was a glorious summer across the south east of England, and in the coastal Kent town of Queensmouth the sun's battery was fully charged, birds were chirping, parks were green like a freshly re-clothed snooker table full of kids using their cue like legs to kick balls around. Minus the graffiti, council estates, down and outs drinking on benches and the litter lining the streets and beach, it was reminiscent of a colourful cartoon land.

Michael lived in his parents' house, which was in one of the nicer parts of town. The houses all had at least three bedrooms, their own driveways, and huge back gardens. The community here were not poor, scruffy or scummy, neither were they rich, spoilt and snobby, they sat happily between the social classes.

Michael's room was typical of a twenty-five-year-old man who had not yet moved out from his parents. The walls were scattered in posters of classic movie posters, clothes lived in two places; the floor and the clothes rack. In one corner sat his forty-inch television on a black TV stand with his game console underneath, video games scattered next to it. It was too much effort to put them back in the case when changing game. His most important picture sat on his desk and was of him and his girlfriend Tara. It was his favourite photo of the two of them. Piercing sky blue eyes, nicely brushed back brown hair and a cute button nose. He did not think she looked too bad in it either, eyes so green that no matter the time of year you would be permanently reminded of Spring whenever you looked into them. Michael was stood behind her as his chin rested on top of her blonde hair, he looked comfortable as if he was resting on a silk blanket, the picture was taken on a camping trip two years' prior, the moon glaring down on both of them gave them an ambience of a match made in heaven.

"You know that picture of you and Tara looks like you are both about to be abducted by aliens?" said Tom, sat on Michaels unmade bed. He had visited to help Michaels dig out part of the back garden in preparation for a pond to be installed. Tom was not only quite a bit shorter than his friend but he was also wider, a build that helped him play rugby in his youth, though muscle was slowly starting to manifest into a beer belly. His hair was short round the sides and swept to the side on top, at the moment he was clean shaven but was constantly going through a weekly tradition of growing a beard, it turning ginger, then he shaved it off. Someone had just pointed out to him the day before that it had turned ginger and promptly reached for the shaving foam.

"What's wrong with you today?" Michael said spinning in his office chair to meet Tom's gaze "Is it because I have asked you to help me with my Mums garden? Because you did offer"

"Do you not know what day it is?" Tom arose from the bed much like his voice.

"Of course I do, it has been tough on all of us, but don't take it out on me and Tara"

Tom realised his outburst was a bit of an overreaction and sat back down on the bed, but his face showed pure contempt for his mate and was not about to let the accusation of it being tough on both of them slide.

"Tough?" Tom was much calmer now but his tone had a teaspoon of sarcasm "I'm the mug that became single two weeks before the ban came into effect and have somehow managed to abstain from pulling a girl ever since, and it hasn't been through the lack of trying! I'm the guy who was spoilt by the internet so much that my fragile little mind can't even use imagination to aid in my alone time, I'm…"

"What are you getting at" Michael decided to interrupt Tom before he divulged too much information that would haunt him for the rest of his life.

"I haven't had any sexual release in a year" Michael realised he had failed as Tom blurted this out. "At least you have Tara there for you, truly I'm happy for you, but that doesn't help me"

"But as I have said, it's not all rainbows for me, With Tara at University I have to go without sex term at a time and she can't even send me raunchy pictures like she used to" Michael was trying his best to relate to Tom's predicaments.

"There's ways round that" Tom said with a smile as he placed a hand on Michaels shoulder. Michael looked confused at how Tom now seemed to think he was the one helping the other "What you do is get her to send you a picture of her eating a banana. It would do it for me."

"This is exactly the reason you are still single." Michael had tried the nice approach, but now it was time to tease his best friend "Maybe you will be better off heading to one of them dodgy brothels. I hear they are popping up all over the place since the ban, I'm sure there must be one here in Queensmouth by now"

"There always has been" Tom said "above Sammi's pizza along the seafront." Michael quivered as he glanced at the empty 'Sammi's' pizza box greasily resting on top of his waste bin in the corner of his room. He hoped now, more than ever, that the employees washed their hands "and now you have mobile brothels, camper vans that will turn up in supermarket car parks at night. Both are far too expensive. These businessmen know what they are doing, ripping us off. Plus Tom Does not pay for Sex!" Tom added somewhat offended, and had to remind Michael that before the ban he was a notorious womanizer.

"Well maybe you should, get out there and go back to being the old Tom huh? You're always talking to girls when you are out, maybe don't get so drunk and go seal the deal." Michael made a valid statement of which Tom knew was right. He hated it when Michael was right yet it happens so often, he was Tom's voice of reason. Still Tom's stubbornness would not allow him to admit this and instead he sat grinding his teeth.

"Have you two lost the use of your hands?" Michael and Tom nodded at each other both appreciating the relatable but unintentional innuendo that had just come out of Michael's Mum's mouth as she stood on his bedroom doorway. "I thought you two would have had the hole dug for the pond by now, your Dad never bothered to dig it up for me and now you Mikey are doing the same. Bloody bone-idle men in my life…" with a rant in full effect the two friends took the hint and left the bedroom with Michael's mother following with her rambling still within earshot. At the bottom of the stairs the boys decided to turn right into the living room where the TV was playing a mid-morning tabloid talk show todays subject was about a man whose wants his wife to take a lie detector test, as she sat sobbing holding three children, of three different Ethnicities. Michaels mum took the bait and whilst Tom and Michael carried on through to the dining room, she caught a glimpse of the topic and collapsed onto the sofa.

"Ok we really need to get started on the pond." Michael said looking out of the glass doors that gave access to his parents back garden. "I don't want to have to listen to that again and I'm sure Dad will appreciate the old girl being calm for dinner later." Tom nodded in agreement and they set off to the bottom of the long garden. They peered into next doors garden showing the neighbour's almost exotic yard in contrast. You could hear the tinkling of the new cherub water feature as the child spat water into the air, landing in the middle of a freshly sprung pond, with giant golden nuggets of fish darting from one side to the other. Despite the increase in cat related fish homicide, Michael's mother was insistent that their garden must implement its own water feature.

"You know them World war two films where they dig big tunnels to escape prisoner of war camps?" Tom shouted as he chucked Michael a shovel and threw his over his shoulder like a gun "we totally should dig our way to the pub, this is already proving hard work"

"We haven't even made it to the end of the garden, yet alone start digging" Michael retorted with a chuckle, he too fancied a beer and knew Tom was just jesting, as they approached the far end of the garden they scanned the scenery and without much contemplation settled on a central spot to slam them shovels into.

"X Marks the spot." They both exclaimed.

After nearly two hours of meticulous digging in the basking sun the hole was deep enough and wide enough that a dying elephant could easily use it as a final resting place and the sweat dripping off of each man could have produced enough water to fill the pond as well as provide a suitable environment for the tropical fish Michael's mother was talking about getting. This was the moment Michael had decided to head back into the kitchen to grab a couple of well-deserved succulent beers, to refuel whilst Tom was left to his own devices. Realising he was by himself Tom decided, as was his nature, that he was not going to put in more effort than his partner and instead half assed a couple of digs before looking over his shoulder and pulling his phone from his pocket, started to check his text messages. He was leaning on his shovel whilst checking his phone when he heard the noise of feet trampling on the gravel, he panicked thinking Michael would catch his slacking off so he started digging quickly as if he was looking for oil. He was relieved when the rustling was just that of a cat chasing a butterfly, but it was enough of a warning and combined with the lack of signal on his phone he decided to dig, and dig a lot.

Michael knew Tom too well and as he stood in the kitchen reaching for the coldest of cans he assumed Tom would be taking a break, lazing, then pretending, upon Michaels return to have been hard at it the whole time. However, after the hard work both had already put into digging this pond he could not begrudge him having a can of lager. However, he was not going to let him get away with it that easily and as he took two cans of beer out of the fridge the one in his strongest left hand he shook to its core. He could not wait to see the beer explode in Tom's face and thought it would ironically cool him down. He quickly popped his head into the living room just to make sure his Mum was still engrossed with the TV and would not come out to interfere before heading back out into the wilderness. He saw Tom at the far end of the garden sitting down legs dangling in the empty pond reading a newspaper

"You lazy bastard" Michael shouted out to his friend, he made sure to give the can in his left hand a couple more shakes as punishment for his slacking. As he got closer he noticed Tom's face had the kind of glow to it that you would normally attribute to a pregnant woman or a bride on their wedding day. Although Tom's jaw was drooping, you could tell he was also smiling and wholly besotted in what he was reading and had failed to see Michael arrive with the beers. When Michael was close, he could see what Tom was fixated on and he dropped both cans of lager in shock. With the cans crashing on the gravel, Tom exited his reverie, snapped back to reality, and looked up at Michael with the biggest smile and a tear in his eye.

"They… They are beautiful." For the first time in a year both Michael and Tom were glancing at a pornographic image, it was one of Michael's father's dirty magazines, Michael was not sure if it was one he recognised back when he discovered his fascination for breasts at thirteen years old. He glanced to the soil-covered suitcase that Tom had obviously pulled from their freshly dug pond. It was full to the rim with magazines and DVD's, their covers a collage of nakedness. The pond was now hosting an orgy. Michael's father had obviously pulled a bait and switch when they attended their local porn-burning bonfire. This explained why digging up the pond did not prove as difficult as it should have, but what did Michael's dad incinerate instead of his explicit content. In addition, what were they to do it with it now the discovery had been unearthed? One thing was for sure they really had struck oil.

CHAPTER 2

Holly was appropriately dressed all in black to accompany the quietness of the occasion. It was not a funeral; it was a Saturday afternoon in a traditionally busy pub, named 'the Bunker'. Saturday afternoons as of late had rightfully become known as the graveyard shift. Noon until two was survivable; the old boys would play dominoes in one corner, getting far too amped up about losing coppers, which always made Holly laugh. How someone could get so happy about winning twenty pence when they had spent a hundred times that on beer already in that afternoon baffled her but at least they were cheerful. The wives would often stroll in one by one to meet their husbands over the course of the afternoon, it was more of a symbolic last orders warning to the chaps than anything else and they never stayed for more than a half of bitter once they had arrived. Holly found it sweet, how could these marriages survive fifty, sixty, maybe seventy years? It was truly a different generation, maybe a time when soul mates really did exist. Caught in thought she wondered whether any of these pensioners were in the world war two bunker of which the pub took its name from. The story goes that an Anderson shelter once stood where the pub was, an infamous one that provided alcohol for its occupants. After the war ended the tin shack was still popular, predominantly amongst married men sneaking out for a pint when the pubs used to close for their mandatory couple of hours in the afternoons, it was also the last place their wives would think of looking. When the wives and authorities found out about the establishment the owner of the shelter tried his luck at building and running his own public house, and 'The Bunker' has remained since the late forties, also remaining in the family. The Person who founded the pub was Holly's great Grandad Charlie.

Noon until two was not just a residential care home; it also had a fair share of younger families coming in to play pool and join in the lunchtime meat raffle and enjoy a casual drink before the riff raff of the night arrive. The evenings were just as good if not better. There was always something going on, pub quizzes, karaoke and many functions, it was never more than a fortnight without a birthday party, wedding reception or wake to bring in the drinkers. The pub was also a popular starting off point for groups of lads and lasses before entering the epileptic danger zone known as Queensmouth's clubbing nightlife. Holly did not work the nightshifts; she was glad on one hand because it meant she could be one of the people enjoying their Saturday night shenanigans. However, on the other one, her shift was two until six, which until the month of June came along were a barrel of laughs to work and more importantly led to more barrels of beer sold. Unlike the introduction of the smoking ban ten years earlier, the erotic entertainment ban did not have an adverse effect on the pub trades. In fact, more people were being driven to drink in attempts to seduce potential partners which Holly herself was no stranger to being the subject of. She had been single since before the ban, so she occasionally enjoyed being the subject of desire from time to time. Not that she would ever let the customers know that.

Instead, the ghost town this saloon had now become was mainly due to the football season ending and as the landlord, Holly's father, stated that it was because of it being "one of them fucking stupid between years" where there was no World cup, European championships, a lack of cricket, rugby, Olympics or other sporting occasions led to barren Saturday afternoons.

It was five past two when the dominoes went away for the day and their wives escorted the last of the dinosaurs into a temporary extinction for the week.

"You've got to be impressed with your husband's ladies, they are walking better than I will be twelve hours later" This comment bought smiles and chuckles from the elderly collective and as they said goodbye Holly was showered with compliments of how sweet she was, how funny, and if the blokes were sixty years younger how they would court her. Holly's smile was unfeigned as she exchanged goodbyes with the punters. Their voices got quieter the further down the corridor to the pubs front door they went until the slam of the heavy metal front door left Holly alone.

This was when the graveyard shift really began. Two in the afternoon until five in the evening, which is the time when the regulars of the Bunker find it appropriate to start their Saturday night drinking. Conversing with staff members from other pubs, Holly discovered this was the average start time among the regulars at Queensmouth's other establishments.

There was only so many times Holly could exit the horseshoe shaped bar and walk around straightening chairs and collecting the few empty glasses that remained, she made sure snacks were adequately stocked up, the fridge was full of bottles and the bar area and tables were clean. Alone she slumped against the bar leaning her chin into her palm which scrunched up her face, her other hand obtained the television remote. She slowly flicked through the music channels looking for anything to help her get through this shift. She was thankful as she stumbled upon the dance music station. The bass beat on the song sent Holly bouncing upright and before she knew it, she was in the mood for the weekend. Dancing randomly around the bar she lifted one of her short legs up onto the bar, rotating her curvaceous hips in a hypnotising way, moving her shoulders in rhythm with her head, it was

14

the confidence of being alone that let her shine and fully embrace her well-hidden inner diva.

She stood to attention just before she let her guard down entirely, the best thing about it being empty in this pub was that no one could sneak in without Holly knowing, the slam of the front door gave ample warning to get back on task.

Holly was annoyed to see it was not a customer but instead a delivery man wanting access to the pub cellar, after delivering two steel drums of lager he was in his truck and on his way leaving Holly to her own devices again. She looked at the clock.

"You have got to be shitting me." She was aware she was swearing at an inanimate object, but the clock read quarter to three. The tick tock of the clock was mocking her as she continued her tirade, "Move faster, I'm warning you or I'm putting up a digital clock" It was when she noticed her fist waving at the clock that she turned and looked into the mirror behind the bar "I'm going mad." She confessed.

The mirror was the distraction she needed, sod it she thought, and she started playing with her hair in different styles, untying her pulled back shiny black hair letting it dangle in front of her round, smooth face. After doubting the other styles, she settled for tying it in a nice neat bun before really treating herself and covering her lips with a bright red lipstick and applying her make-up for the night. Then she added her piece de resistance, a red bandanna that matched the lipstick and contrasted her light blue eyes, making both stand out more. She lacked self-confidence and did not think of herself as attractive but she knew from experience the men that would be in later would like it.

Then she remembered the last time she wore the bandana. Tom, one of her favourite customers, a peer at school, yet probably the one customer that infuriated her the most had a remark to make about the headpiece.

"Who have you come as, a gangsta rapper?" was his witty aside the last time she wore the bandana. The two had a love hate relationship, he loved to buy beer and wind Holly up, and Holly hated being on the end of his teasing statements. She knew it was banter and the world's worst kept secret was that he had a huge crush on her, he had admitted as much to her father one night when he was intoxicated. She had often contemplated giving him a chance, even if they were the same height of five foot seven, she preferred her men taller but Tom was handsome and rugged, yet he did himself no favours to convince Holly to take that chance.

He was a walking Oxymoron, a man who claims he wants to settle down yet flits from job to job on impulse, a man who wants a steady relationship but spends every weekend drinking and trying to get into the pants of any woman with a pulse. He would make loud statements about being in the biggest dry patch of his life sexually which further failed to endear him to Holly. The Erotic entertainment act did not diminish his confidence, but it increased his frustration and as that increased so did how desperate he looked.

Staring at herself in the mirror she started contemplating putting the hair down and removing the make-up but that was short lived as the booming bang of the front door closing interrupted her trail of thought. What followed next were the voices of two men, getting louder as they approached the bar, they were in deep debate, using words such as 'mid-off' and 'googly' Holly was clueless as to what they were engaged in conversation about, she only worked out it was about cricket once the word was actually uttered.

"Cricket talk on a Saturday guys, really?" That was Holly's way at welcoming the locals back into their domain; she whipped a towel over her shoulder and instinctively started pouring up a strong lager and a not so strong one for Adam and Simon respectively. Adam was only just a tad bit taller than Holly but the size of his arms and chest complete with tribal tattoos bulging from his black t-shirt made her look small.

"Sorry Hol, take one for yourself to." Holly smiled and thanked Adam for the drink and said she would save it for after her shift when she was allowed to have some strong stuff. She was already thinking about the vodka and coke.

"Looking good today Hol." Adams ginger lanky partner in crime, Simon said being honest, his blue shirt was done up to his big bulging Adams apple. Holly smiled gratefully, almost embarrassed. She struggled to accept compliments in public. The lads took their change before turning away from the bar and sitting at their favourite table. They added three more seats around it in preparation for the rest of their entourage to arrive.

Adam and Simon set the pace as people slowly trickled into the pub; Holly now had to pour drinks, a pleasant change to the lack of atmosphere and boredom from earlier. Next, to enter were Andy and Gary. Two more of the bunker's regulars, men in their mid-forties and definitely past their peak in appearance. Gary was bald, Andy had thickly gelled and obviously dyed black hair and wore glasses, both rested their well-formed beer bellies against the bar. What they lacked as eye candy they made up for with old stories, fantastic humour and general knowledge that always won them the pub quizzes, they perched themselves on wooden bar stools.

The pilgrimage to the pub continued, next was a chap, who once he acquired his drink, went and sat at the fruit machine pouring in coin after coin, then winning some, just to put it back, and thus was his circle of life only parting from it to get another beverage.

Next was an Indian man nicknamed 'Kneecap'. His real name was Nadeem but his friends dubbed him kneecap because his surname, Patel, sounded like Patella, it was logical and illogical at the same time, he was Indian only in heritage and complexion and spoke in the same cockney like but not really cockney accent the rest of Queensmouth's population did. He was dressed smartly in a recently ironed white shirt with black trousers and gleaming black shoes ready to attempt to use his cheesy charm on the girls down the seafront later, it seldom worked. As he ordered his usual blue alcopop Holly teased him for his beverage choice. He did not understand the criticism and went and sat with Adam and Simon, where he was hastily teased again, sure enough his next drink was a pint of lager.

That is how the trend stayed for the next couple of hours as people wandered in like the animals from Noah's ark. During this time Michael and Tom walked into the pub, Holly prepared herself to go one more round with Tom's barrage of banter. She approached the bar ready to spar and was shocked as Tom walked the full horseshoe of the bar straight to the table with Adam, Simon and kneecap.

"Holly" Michael called out to Holly who was occupied by the surprise of the boycott from Tom. "Can I have two pints please?"

"Sorry Mikey." Holly had known Michael for years; their respective fathers bought them up side by side in this very pub and they had been the subject of a drunken arranged marriage when they were toddlers which blossomed into a lifelong friendship. She had also introduced him to Tara, a friend of her younger sister and she thought the couple were well suited "I'm just not used to Tom not having something to say, he didn't even look at me."

"We've both had a long day," Michael said reaching for the two pints and began to walk away from the bar.

"But he didn't even look at my arse as he walked past; this is Tom we're talking about." Holly joked but she may as well have been talking to a mannequin, as Michael looked on, preoccupied by Tom and the rest of his friends sat around like knights at a banquet. Michael left swiftly after receiving his drinks forgetting his usual manners and thanking Holly for the drinks. Holly turned to one of the patrons "That was unusual! What's up with them two?" she inadvertently chose to converse with the one customer entranced by the flashing lights of the fruit machine, who paid her no response or acknowledgment. "Wow my invisibility powers are on peak performance today." She complained to nobody.

Thankfully, the rest of the customers were friendlier and for the rest of her shift Holly was privy to being the subject of being flirted with, chatted to others, and even got into a conversation with Andy and Gary about which was better Star Wars or Star Trek, she said she liked the one with the green thing in it. Yet her intrigue kept bringing her back to the conference going on over at the lad's table especially as all she could hear was a lot of whispering and looking over shoulders as Tom took centre stage. Holly could not make out what the topic of conversation was but the reactions from Kneecap, Adam and Simon suggested that they did not believe whatever bullshit he was spouting now, Holly mused that it served him right. Their attitude of denial seemed to shift gear when Tom pulled a small white plastic bag from inside his light blue shirt.

"What are you doing? I can't believe you bought it" Michael screamed so Holly didn't have to lip read. The bag was passed around the table all five men were eager to shield whatever was in that bag. This just made Holly more suspicious of all the secrecy as one by one their eyes lit up like headlights. People ordering more drinks distracted Holly's curiosity. While she was bending over into the chiller to get a couple of cold bottles of beer, the five men were up from their seats, making their way around the bar and towards the exit. As they left, Simon whispered into the ears of Andy and Gary and they too joined the mass walk out by waddling behind.

This now left the bunker a third empty and Holly was baffled as to what had just gone on. Her mood lifted when she looked up at the clock and could not help but smile when she could see that in ten minutes, her replacement would be in and Holly's tenure behind the bar would be finished for one night. Most importantly, she could now go and get drunk with her girlfriends.

CHAPTER 3

The sun was just starting to go down on this fine summer's day. Seven grown men of all shapes, sizes, ages and hairlines were walking down the side of Michael's house, through a wooden gate and into the garden, the sound of all their feet crunched in unison on the pebbles like a marching parade troops leaving their families to go fight for their country. As they reached the far end of the long garden Tom pointed in the direction of a large mud pit, the scurried around and all stared down into the hole half expecting to see an Australian wave back at them.

Michael looked down cautiously, and then up at the back windows of his house.

"I can't believe we're doing this." He said peering through a gap in his fingers. Michael had complained the whole way; his parents were out but he still used disturbing them as an excuse not to head to his garden. The reality of his cowardice was that he was worried about the ramifications of being caught with pornography, what if they were seen by neighbours or heard by passers-by. The biggest dread was that one of the gentlemen in the garden would be a snake and report their findings to authorities. Criminal charges surrounding illegal pornography were rare, but those that were reported made mainstream news and the cases were, without fail, classed as high profile. Those found guilty were made an example of, a warning to anyone else about breaking this relatively new law; Heavy fines and custodial sentences were handed out to anyone caught in possession of pornographic material.

A buoyed Tom took a leap into the hole he had created hours earlier, landing with a triumphant thump. His smile was plain to see as he wiped off soil and removed the plastic sheeting him and Michael used to hide the blue suitcase from sight and reached for the zip of the case. He looked up with a grin delaying and teasing the onlookers.

"Get on with it" rang out from the mouths of the groaning onlookers, including Michael. The setting sun gave the contents of the case an ominous glow and Tom opened it the full way to gasps, then speechlessness.
The silence of the seven was slowly broken as few words began to utter from their mouths.

"Glorious" Said Andy trying to focus through the lenses of his glasses.

"I can't believe it is true," added his bald headed companion Gary "I can see stuff I remember owning when I was a teenager in the seventies."

"It's been so long" Adam contributed, the man with the biggest arms of the group, seemed most likely to weep tears of joy.

"They're… They're…."

"TIT'S" Shouted Simon interrupting Kneecap, his long ginger frame leaning closely to the porno pit with his giraffe like neck. Each comment added to Michael's paranoia. Twitching and continuing to scout his surroundings, his shushing of Simon's outburst was ironically the loudest noise in the garden.

Meanwhile Tom was standing in his hole, behind the suitcase, a fist resting on either side of his hips, proud like a new parent, or as proud as the time he managed to flip and catch fifty beer mats one handed.

"Look, just look, Mikey's old man must have really been neglected in the bedroom to amass this much." Tom was blossoming.

"Did he never use the internet? I don't think I ever used anything else?" Adam said laughing at the primitive form of porn "Using this would be like whacking one out to a cave painting." Simon stood tall laughing from Adams remark, the cocktail of laughing and standing up too quick gave him a head rush.

"It's the only reason I got a laptop to be honest." Gary confessed with Andy nodding in agreement and adding.

"Well, and to gamble without having to trek to the bookies." Michael eased a bit and loosened up, even letting out a small laugh, the benevolence bought him to a zone of relaxation as Tom again took the limelight.

"But look at what we actually have here" He began picking up samples then dropping them back into the suitcase to pick up another to show off "We have magazines, from vintage stuff to some released just before the ban, we have videos, not that anyone owns a VCR player these days, and look DVD's so many DVD's. I haven't had a chance to sort through them yet but look how many different fetishes and genres we have." At this point Tom had both hands full waving his arms as if he was holding a handful of bank notes from a successful heist.

"I will give you twenty quid right now to buy big black butts twenty-three." Adam proposed whipping his wallet out of his pocket quicker than a cowboy pulling his gun from a holster. Tom went to complete the transaction picking up the DVD and reaching up towards Adam's gigantic outstretched arm. Michael intervened jumping between the two men's arms and into the pit, wrestling the DVD from Toms grasp and dropping it back into the suitcase. Tom and Michael argued about the legality of this whilst more offers chimed in from the other five men as if they were at an auction.

After much persuasion Michael managed to convince all involved that this will be discussed further, but for now they should all leave his garden and head to the nightclub down the seafront, the reminder of free entry and half price drinks before nine o'clock was enough to convince them to head back down the long garden and off of Michaels property.

Andy and Gary were left standing at the hole staring down, oblivious to the fact the rest had started to leave.

"Is it bad that we are standing here mesmerized by this?" Gary pondered not breaking his trail of sight.

"What's the difference between this and a group of people staring at the statue of David at an exhibition? It's all art." Andy replied, also not bothering to look at his friend.

"Well I would start with the awkward boners." with Gary's retort both immediately looked straight ahead and said nothing more, the moment was broken by Michaels annoyance.

"Come on Grandads, get out of my garden," he yelled and both of the older men complied roaming wildly towards the gate. After saying goodbye to the five young lads Andy and Gary headed back to the bunker to finish their pints, taking a trip down memory lane discussing their favourite erotic media memories and how downloading the playboy bunny of the month in the nineties was one slow painful strip tease. The rest headed off on the ten-minute trek towards the seafront of Queensmouth, where they planned to drink, dance, and embarrass themselves until the early hours of the morning.

A little after midnight and the party was in full swing, strobe lighting made the dance floor look like an intergalactic space battle, a stench of sweat and perfume surrounded the nightclub as people flung themselves around, lost in a world of hypnotic music and alcohol. Kneecap had reached the point where he took advantage of his cultural heritage to win a dance off. He used dance moves such as his hands pressed together above his head moving them like a snake, and leaping from foot to foot, he self-taught himself to dance from the various weddings his large family dragged him to over the years, but after various shots of vodka he was in his element, the self-proclaimed Bollywood Billy Elliot.

Also in their element were Adam and Simon, they had reached that point of intoxication where they felt irresistible to women, unaware the drunker they got the more their charm wore thin, however their success rate was above average, part of that was due to Adams keen eye for the more voluptuous lady. After a drink, he always made a beeline for those of a larger persuasion. On this night he danced behind an overweight girl, with a pretty face, well made up, with blonde hair and green eyes. He placed a hand on each side of her waist stroking her tight white t-shirt and she gyrated along with him in, Simon as usual then went for the kill with one of her friends. He chose a stick thin, red head, however if Simon was the tallest in the club, she was by far the shortest. The long distance between their voices made their getting to know each other chat look more like an argument, and when they got round to kissing each other Simon looked like a mother bird feeding her offspring.

Michael swaggered out of the toilet, half in motion to the music and half due to being on his eighth beer. He surveyed the situation on the dance floor; his love and loyalty to Tara prevented him from going and joining Adam and Simon on hunting season. In addition, while he liked a dance, seeing the shapes Kneecap was throwing up made him suddenly self-aware of what his own dancing would look like. Michael was startled as Holly, like a female jack in the box sprung up in front of him.

"You need to speak to Tom I'm worried" she slurred; Holly was still in the same black get up she was wearing whilst on her shift at the Bunker but one eye was now wonky as it suffered from what her father called wine wandering eye syndrome. "Not once has he spoke to me or anyone since he got here, I even got some of my girlfriends to go and flirt with him, but nothing! He looks broken." She waved her glass of wine in the general direction of the bar where Tom was standing with a bottle of beer to the left of him as he elbows rested on the bar. This was not through the effects of alcohol though and he was far from drunk. He had acquired a pen from one of the bar staff and was meticulously scribbling on a beer mat, stopping occasionally deep in thought or to count on his fingers. Michael was intrigued and had just assumed Tom stayed at the bar to flirt outrageously with the barmaids as per usual, but this was different, he assured Holly he would go and figure out what was wrong with Tom.

At the behest of her girlfriends and the change of song Holly, rushed off onto the dance floor and joined in with a performance that looked like some sort of female mating ritual, the ladies in the club seemed more able to dance in sync, a lot better than the men. No matter how drunk they were. "For once it's the opposite… you haven't had enough to drink" to Toms surprise Michael yanked the beer mat from his grasp "It's a little early to be worrying about your fantasy football team Tommo, what witty name have you gone for this year?"

Tom snatched the beer mat back, his nose flared with annoyance; he took a swig of Michael's beer as an act of revenge, before Michael pulled his beer back with the same scornful look.

"It's a business plan, and further more you know my team name is always named Crystal Phallus" Tom folded the beer mat and placed it into the chest pocket of his blue shirt, he contemplated for a second "Is this the most coherent I've ever been at this time?"

"It's also one of the only times you have ever used a three syllable word, I thought we discussed this nonsense mate, selling" Michael looked around "you know that it is illegal."

Tom then grabbed his own warmed up bottle of beer and started to peel the label off it, before taking a gulp and exhaling.

"Michael, we are sitting on a gold mine, we have so much variety and such a high quantity, we could make a fortune, we obviously have clientele available already. How quick was Adam in offering us money?"

"We'll be sitting on a prison sentence if caught."

"Look at alcohol" Tom held his bottle arm's length in front of him ready to use as a prop like Hamlet and Yorick's skull. "Some people like beer, some like whiskey, some like alcopops, we don't get why they do, but it's their choice and we respect that! It's the same thing with porn, different needs but everybody enjoys a session, now you can't tell me porn is any worse for society than alcohol" Tom placed the bottle down and leered directly into Michaels bewildered eyes, "Can you?"

"Even horny, drunk Tom is less deluded than you are now, I'm going over to the dance floor, get some drink down you and join us when you're ready." Michael grooved his way over to the horde on the dance floor and was lost in the sea of waving arms, the next time he glanced over at the bar Tom was gone.

CHAPTER 4

His voice was slurred. The words were wrong. Nevertheless, there was no denying the tune of Bohemian Rhapsody being murdered by Michael as he stumbled front, back, and side-to-side along his avenue. It was a tradition of the group to sing drunkenly in the early hours of the morning after a night out. Michael, Adam, Kneecap and Simon started singing it just before Michael veered off onto the road his house stood. It was their fourth collaboration of the journey but now as Michael approached his front door, he carried it on solo.

Michael reached into his trouser pocket and realised he didn't have a key. No big deal he shrugged to himself, there was always a plan B and he opened the wooden gate to the side of the house and headed into his back garden all the while continuing his attempt at singing. He got the words wrong replacing monstrosities with 'Pork sausages'. Picking up the hedgehog ornament that guarded the back entrance to his abode he then took three attempts at using his other arm as a fishing rod trying to catch the key waiting under the hedgehog, it took another three attempts to get the key into the lock before a light bulb shined on from an external sensor light at the same time a great idea entered his mind.

With the cheeky grin of a naughty child, he turned and headed towards the end of his garden, shouting for Tara even though his girlfriend was a good couple of hundred miles away and there was no possibility of her hearing him.

"Tara, oh Tara, I'm drunk, I need loving, and where are you?" he stood on a spot in the middle of his garden where the grass turned to gravel, his arms stretched out spinning a full rotation looking for a lover he knew was not near. "Up at your poxy University that's where you are!"

A yellow light beamed from above as Michael's father stood, his eyes wanting to be back shut; his thinning bed hair stood high as if he had slept with his finger in a plug socket, the light from the bedroom bounced off the centre of his exposed bald spot like a lighthouse beacon.

"Michael, it's three in the morning, shut the fuck up."

"Hello father." Michael howled at the light as if it were the moon.

"You're pissed" His father said stating the obvious.

"Where's Tara?" Michael replied with puppy dog eyes.

"She's probably passed out at a desk over working too hard on an essay trying to make something of herself. Not realising her boyfriend is drunk off his arse waking up the whole fucking street" Michael couldn't help but raise an eyebrow at the irony of his foul mouthed father accusing him of waking up the street when he was being ten times louder. Motioning with his thumb back towards the house, he continued, "Now get in the house, so we can all get some sleep"

"I'll be up in two seconds," Michael hiccupped whilst he thought carefully about what he was going to say next. "I really need to go; I'll be up after I've had a leak."

Exhausted Michael's dad closed the window and shuffled away and the bedroom light flicked off leaving complete darkness apart from the stars in the clear night sky. Michael staggered towards the bottom end of the garden edging closer to the newly dug pond. In reality, he did not need to pee at all, he found three bushes more than adequate to use during the walk home. What he really needed was his Girlfriend with him to sort out this horny drunkenness. That was not possible, but what was possible was the next best thing, the forbidden fruit. Pornography.

It went against his moral fibres, and he was proud of all the hard work Tara was doing trying to get a degree, yet in his drunken state he felt deprived of his girlfriend. His intoxicated state however did not entirely rid him of his wariness and worry. As he got closer to the buried treasure he was more conscious of being loud and tip toed the final few steps. He carefully pulled back the grey plastic sheeting covering the pond and decided he was going to reach in blindly and settle for the first magazine in his grasp and sneak it upstairs, Tom would be proud of him.

Michael kept slapping dirt with each reach unsuccessfully finding a magazine whilst blind, he had to open an eye to see what he was doing. What he saw was grotesque and immediately sobered him up, inside the pond was nothing. Looking at his own empty grave Michael decided the best course of action was to go to sleep and worry about this predicament in the morning, even though he knew sober Michael would not appreciate it.

A few hours later Michael woke up with a headache partly because of a hangover, partly because of the incident that gave him nightmares in his sleep. All that pornography missing, hundreds of DVD's and magazines just upped and vanished. That was naïve of him to think that and he knew it, he knew that the only possible explanation was theft. He had never sprung out of bed with so much energy after a night of drinking before; neglecting to shower or do his hair, he ripped a grey tracksuit off his clothes rack and changed quicker than they change the tyres at a pit stop. He grabbed his phone from his bedside table and tried to call Tom

"I warned him this would happen" he said waiting for his friend to pick up the phone, annoyed at no answer he pressed the call button again "What did I say, if word of this got out, we would end up in trouble, what if the police found it?" He was overthinking and Tom was not answering, he decided he wasn't going to bare this burden alone, this is all Tom's fault he thought, after smelling the stale alcohol on his breath he quickly brushed his teeth before sprinting down the stairs, grabbing his car keys and heading out of the front door. As he had time to think he decided it was not worth the risk to drive and posted his car key back through the front door before he set off on a jog to Tom's house.

The journey was not too long, jogging it took ten minutes; the route was almost second nature to Michael yet this morning he was so focussed he did not notice anything going on around him. He forgot to look right whilst hopping across a busy road narrowly avoiding a collision with a red car driven by an old woman, whose glasses only peeked above the steering wheel. He was oblivious to the groundsman at the local cricket ground saying good morning leaving the older man bewildered as Michael zoomed past. Running up a hill towards a primary school his heart pounded and was asking him if a moments rest would be such a bad idea, however in his own mind there was not a minute to waste.

The scenery soon got greyer the further he raced past the beach, the train station represented the divide in class, literally the other side of the tracks, as cafes were replaced by arcades and kids skipping along the seafront turned to tracksuit wearing hoodlums with no place other to loiter. Graffiti took prominence on the walls, and one pub was already open for breakfast yet that did not stop the local alcoholic community from sipping their second beers of the day.

Turning down an alley created the start of a gritty obstacle race, the cracks and potholes in the pavement were unsettling enough without having to weave and dodge copious amounts of dog shit. He vaulted, first an abandoned mattress followed by a black sack full of rubbish, he barged through a green wooden gate that led into a back garden where the grass was standing almost at knee height, and Michael entered a backdoor leading to a staircase that he puffed up leading to the front door of Tom's flat. His heart was beated as hard as his fist banged on the front door.

Tom answered the door, half-naked with no shame; he was still wearing the blue shirt from the night before, although undone revealing his gold chain tangled in his chest hair. He was wearing yellow and green boxer shorts with the word POW wrote across the front in red lettering, almost as red were his eyes, an indicator of a hangover or tiredness and Michael knew Tom had hardly consumed any alcohol the night before.

"I warned you didn't I?" Tom wretched his face at Michael's statement, as if to say it was too early for this, he made a caveman like grunt and turned down his hallway into his small kitchen. Michael was following close behind pointing aggressively at Tom's back, steam pouring from his ears "We should have just re buried it all, but oh no, you had to tell everyone, hell not just tell them, you showed them where it was, that's like telling the hairy armed bloke that runs the kebab shop where we keep the sheep…. What are you doing?" Michael's rant was interrupted by Tom's actions.

"Making my speciality" Tom was letting Michael's words go in one ear and out of the other as he added milkshake powder to his cereal making his patented Strawberry Cornflakes; he offered some up to Michael but that only seemed to agitate him further and Michael swatted it away like an annoying fly.

"Why are you not listening to me?" Michael reached boiling point as Tom once again walked past him, he was beginning to question whether he was really there in Tom's flat or if he died from shock last night and was now a less than friendly ghost shouting aimlessly.

"I am" Tom replied after slurping on his spoon "It's just really early and I haven't had any sleep, what's your problem?"

"It's gone!" Michael Yelled.

"Gone?" Tom repeated.

"The Porn."

"The Porn?"

"The porn we dug up!" At the end of his tether, Michael shook Tom, spilling milk.

"Oh" Tom said nonchalantly as he used his elbow to open the door to his living room.

"Oh? Is that all you can say? We could end up in trouble if it's got into the wrong hands, even more so my Dad could be put away" Michael was so pent up he was oblivious to the wooden floor covered in erotic magazines and DVD's laid out neatly, the yellow painted walls of the room giving it a rich glow once again. "It was you?" He exclaimed angrily followed by relief "I have been panicking all night!"

"Well you can stop panicking now" Tom had knelt down with his cereal near his collage of erotic media, picking up a DVD from a pile and deciding where that particular one should be placed. "Hang on a minute, what do you mean all night? Why were you looking for it at that time… ah you dirty boy Mikey."

"What?" protested Michael.

"Was someone missing Tara?"

"Oh shut up Tom." Michael had been caught out and he knew it but he was about to transfer the heat immediately off himself "And you're telling me you behaved with all this at your disposal?"

"I had one, and I tell you if anyone was on the end of that they would have made it to the moon." Michael had to put his head in the palm of his hands disgusted at a remark he bought on himself, Tom was grinning proudly "First time in a year Michael".

"So what is this then?" Michael pointed at the arrangement sitting on the floor where the coffee table would usually be.

"Oh you're interested now? You weren't last night!" Tom slurped away at the last remnants of his breakfast from the bowl.

"I'm quickly trying to change the topic of conversation."

Tom was looking ecstatic to have the opportunity to pitch his plan and he hyperactively explained what lay before them with the same excitement Einstein must have used when he first tried to explain the theory of relativity. He went into detail explaining how first he split the collection into Magazines and discs. Then within those columns each item was then categorised and aged, some of the material crossed into multiple fetishes leading to placements within the two like a Venn diagram. The ages of the DVD's started at fourteen years ago, whereas some of the magazines went back as much as thirty years spanning from the eighties to now. In total, there were twenty-six different categories and Tom explained the variety would help keep things fresh with clients and make it easier to attract new potential customers to lease the pornography to.

As Tom continued Michael was reluctant to concede that he was impressed, he had never seen his oldest friend so invested in something, the closest was when he was filling out his online dating profile or studying the winning form of horses, before handing money over to an ever so grateful bookmaker. Yet Michael could not shrug off the legality of it all, it was a very well-known fact that owning pornography was against the law. He reiterated the heavy fines and short prison sentences that were issued up and down the country, Tom told him he was being silly and being irrational. Michael reminded Tom that these judgments were only for people that were caught in possession of it, heaven forbid what kind of hefty judgement would be passed on a distributor and in Michaels mind, they would be looked at in the eyes of the law in the same vein as drug dealers.

"And how often are you offered pills on a night out down the seafront? And what about people smoking weed for pain relief? Can you begrudge them that?" Michael nodded; he had no comeback for Tom's rationale "So say a man isn't getting any action because his wife is too tired or has a headache, and the frustration is building, is that any different?" Michael tried to interrupt but Tom would not give him a chance "All I'm saying Mikey is, we have been given a chance to offer a service to people who have been deprived, and if we can earn a few quid at the same time well that's fair enough! We already have interest from some of the lads and you know what it's like around here, it's so inbred that word will travel in no time, they pay us to loan our material for a few days then we get it back and loan them some more, it's like a library."

"A Library for perverts" Michael chimed in.

"Exactly, come on you could use the extra money, maybe put it towards a holiday for you and Tara."

"And what would Tara think if she found out how I got this extra cash?"

"Well she's not here at the moment is she; all I say is give it a try."

"And if we get caught?" Michael was trying to map everything out in his mind and be prepped for everything should he be convinced to follow Tom down this path.

"I promise I will fall on the sword" With that last promise Tom was almost certain he had Michael hooked and he extended his hand towards his friend "What do you say, partners?"

Michael was still in two minds and hesitantly sighed before grasping Tom's hand, after all he was loyal to his best friend. Each man tried to squeeze tighter than the other, neither wanting the other to be the Alpha.

"Partners." As soon as the handshake ended, Tom was on his mobile phone ringing around and Michael heard a phrase he never thought he would hear uttered from his friend.

"Adam, can I still interest you in Big Black butts twenty-three?"

CHAPTER 5

"I need a slash." Tom announced to the rest of his friends at the table, before asking them to look after his pint of beer whilst he amended his predicament. He walked through the door to the gent's bathroom which was about as glamorous as you would expect a male toilet to be in a rundown seaside town pub.

"Hey Tom." said another patron as he shook Tom's hand before manoeuvring past him and exiting back towards the bar. It was only after the handshake Tom wondered if the man had washed his hands and looking at his own palm in disgust, decided before he did anything else, he would wash them.

His hand's germ free and smelling of peach he approached the dark blue toilet cubicle door, normally the red symbol indicated it was engaged, and would be reason enough to stop and wait for it to be free. Tom however, upturning the collar of his blue and yellow Striped Queensmouth F.C football shirt braced himself and proceeded to knock on the cubicle door at the same time announcing his own name. That was when the door opened and Tom squeezed into it coming face to face with another man, with the door locked behind them there was not much room for either to have personal space. Tom double-checked the person stood before him just to ensure his trousers were up.

"Just protocol." Tom said to chip away at the ice "Welcome to my office Chris." The man he was facing was a sometime user of the bunker bar although Tom would not class him as a regular; he would use it to watch the big football matches so he did not have to pay for a satellite subscription at home. Tom had chatted to him before and even played him at pool. Chris exchanged pleasantries with Tom although his unusually quiet voice and constant beard scratching were sure signs of him being nervous and uncomfortable.

Tom climbed up on top of the toilet seat moving a ceiling tile up revealing the pipe work and roof of the establishment. He then stepped onto the metal tissue dispenser and used the framework the tiles rested on to propel himself up until he was seated on the framework, leaving Chris sharing a cubicle with Tom's dangling legs.

"Right I have got your order here, One DVD … code AMA12, that's an Amateur couple's film, and someone rented that one last week, he said good things! Particularly the car park scene" Tom shouted down to Chris who nodded up at Tom in the ceiling, pleased that his choice was a popular one. "And a magazine, you didn't specify a type, ok that's a cheaper option but I'm afraid you get what you're given." Tom lent forward in his crawl space up in the ceiling; He was proud of what he had set up in the men's toilets, he had referred to it at his warehouse, factory and lab on different occasions, but whatever he called it, it was discreet. It included two big gym bags, both with their zips padlocked shut, the red and black one contained all of the day's orders, various magazines and DVD's, that had been submitted during the week. The other bag was a purple Adidas one, which was strictly for the customer's returns from last week's orders. Although the Training bags were padlocked shut Tom, at Michaels suggestion, took extra precaution's and through the handles of each bag was a heavy duty metal chain which in turn was wrapped around one of the water pipes up above, and secured with a similarly heavy duty padlock, both would require some powerful bolt cutters to remove.

Pulling a crystal blue binder from the red and black bag, he flipped it open and like a pop-up book, its contents were on show to his eyes only. It was full of plastic wallets, each wallet holding six disks either side. The amateur section, labelled AMA, was near the front of the binder and finding number twelve was just as simple and he removed the disc and placed it straight ahead of himself resting it on the displaced ceiling tile. Putting the crystal blue folder away, he simultaneously retrieved a clear white binder at the speed of two passing trains.

"Right I'm going to get you to help me pick one at random, ok Chris?" Tom said as if he was shouting down a well.

"Not a problem mate." Chris replied, the wait was beginning to bore him and he was now fighting temptation not to tie Tom's shoelaces together.

"Cool, and remember whatever you get, you get. It's the risk you take." Sod that Tom thought to himself, he intended instead to find one of the magazines he thought nobody would ever choose of their own free will, yet still get a few quid for it. "pick a number between one and seventeen" the reply was six but Tom had no interest in retrieving Chris's number, it was all a ruse to stop Chris from becoming suspicious whilst he searched for a magazine he deemed surplus to requirement. Bingo, he thought as his hands stopped searching. Hardcore Harriet's Hairy Hungarian adventure. With an almost evil grin he removed it from its wallet. To Tom's misfortune, curiosity got the better of him and he decided to flick to a random page, rapidly he felt like he eyes were melting and even let out a repulsed scream swiftly regretting his decision to check the gross content.

"Everything alright Tom?" Chris was looking up into the ceiling.

"Yeah, just lost my balance, don't worry" Even Tom could not be that evil and his conscience got the better of him so he put the devil spawn of a magazine back into the binder. He quickly flicked through a couple of magazines nearby before settling on a bog standard softcore magazine. It was mainly filled with topless photos of young upstart models in their underwear, nothing too explicit but Tom figured you get what you pay for. It might have been considered boring to some, but it saved Chris from the horror of Hairy Harriet.

Tom put everything back in its right place and locked it away before placing an arm either side of the metal framework supporting the tiles and slowly lowered himself down until one of his feet rested on the dented metal tissue dispenser and the other was stretched balancing on the toilet seat. He then put the DVD and magazine in his mouth to secure them, Chris offered to take them from Tom but stubbornly Tom would not accept assistance largely because he had not yet received any payment for the goods. He then popped the ceiling tile back in place before hopping down and straightening up his Queenmouth top, and re-flicking up the collar. Chris was face to face with him again, rubbing his hands together eager with anticipation for the supplies hanging from Tom's jaw.

Tom began talking, mumbling, forgetting his mouth was full. He took both items from within his mouth with his right hand and began offering it outwards towards his new customer. Chris was too enthusiastic to receive his goods, however Tom would not let go of the magazine and DVD giving Chris a look implying that he was forgetting something. Chris, slightly embarrassed that excitement got the better or him, clicked his fingers and retrieved a twenty-pound and a five-pound note that were both scrunched up in one of the pockets of his blue track suit bottoms. The moment the money transferred into Tom's meat hook via a handshake his vice like grip released on the DVD and magazine and Chris was free to enjoy his product. Slipping them down the back of his joggers he left the toilets, Tom could hear the chatter of the busy bar for a split second before the doors closed behind Chris.

Washing his hands one more time, Tom proceeded to dry them his favourite way, by using both hand dryers, one hand under each, he said it was the way Jesus would have dried his hands yet it only seemed to amuse him. Returning from the toilets, he re-joined his friends at their table. Michael and Kneecap were talking about upcoming plans; Kneecap had been invited to another wedding for a distant family member he had never met. Michael asked why Kneecap always went to them if they were that much of a nuisance and Kneecap responded that it is just Indian tradition and it kept his mother happy, besides, as a photographer it was a perfect time to network. There was nearly a thousand people at the last one he attended and it even landed him a couple of jobs.

"That's a lot of people! Any of them interested in porn?" Michael and Kneecap were stunned silent at Tom's sudden interjection, Tom looked around worried he had said something wrong, he had a habit of being ignorant when it came to Kneecap's religion and cultural differences but honestly felt bad whenever he did, it was just different to him, apologetically however he carried on. "Sorry do they have like a Bollywood version of porm already?"

"God, I hope not, I hate the unnecessary story in porn as it is, and could you imagine a twenty-minute dance scene before hand as well, it would be time for my arranged wedding before they got to any of the good stuff" Kneecap was laughing, he always took it in good grace. Michael was very clued up and tolerant of other cultures but between Tom, Adam and Simon there was at least one occasion a week where one of them would accidentally put their foot in it, however the more he taught them, the better they got. "Besides, you guys seem to have enough demand as it is" Kneecap continued aware of how busy the bunker was on Saturday lunchtime for the second weekend in a row. "You don't need the Indian market just yet."

"Don't remind me" said Michael suddenly aware that they were the reason that their local was so busy "I'm surprised Holly hasn't said anything about how busy it is."

"That might work in your favour Mike" Kneecap calmed him by placing a hand on Michaels shoulder "She is too busy to worry about that at all, what reason has she got to think that the reason this pub is so busy is because you two have started dealing erotic masturbatory aides?"

The three men surveyed the situation, it had been two weeks since Tom convinced Michael to begin these shenanigans and nearly every man in the pub that afternoon, even more than the week before, were there primarily to purchase pornography from Tom. The turn out last week shocked Michael enough but this was even worse. Tom was right, people did desire it and these two friends were providing that service, Michael again found himself thinking constantly about the legal implications of breaking the law like this, but the happier he saw it made people the less black and white the morality of the situation became. He also enjoyed the extra money, Michael's thoughts were soon stopped as Tom made an astute observation to himself and Kneecap.

"You know I never thought I would be making money by sharing a toilet cubicle with other men" Tom then enjoyed a sip from his pint.

CHAPTER 6

About twenty miles inland of Queensmouth the historic city, and many say the Heart of Kent, Canterbury is situated. It is famous for its prestigious cathedral, which is home to the Archbishop of Canterbury, one of the stalwarts of the ban of erotic entertainment. It is also known for its multi-cultural demographic with thousands of tourists from all over the world pilgrimaging to the city, as well as an abundance of students choosing one of the two universities situated there to carry out their studies. On top of that is a high street and shopping centre that caters for everyone and only quietens down when the shops shut only to then be replaced by the many pubs and clubs open until the early hours of the morning.

Teachers of the Orlando Bloom primary school sat in their messy staff room; a bin full to the rim of rubbish in the corner. Cups, plates and other utensils were left stained and not washed up and a strong stench from the microwave lingered where no one had bothered to clean it out. Yet this remained ignored as they were enjoying their last few moments of freedom before the last lessons of the week. It was Friday afternoon and each of them knew that with a little perseverance in two hours' time they would be childless for the weekend.

Outside the constant noise of children playing; a blend of laughs, screams and cries went silent. The masses of little humans running around in their purple uniforms screeched to a halt. It was the end of the lunch break and as usual the dinner ladies whistle indicated for the children to stop. On the second whistle they lined up in their respective class groups and one by one they were greeted by their teacher and marched into their classroom.

Class 6S were the last to be led off the playground by their teacher Miss Sunderland. She was a petite young woman with her blonde hair straightened down resting on her shoulders; she had small but bright green eyes and an ever so slightly upturned nose. Her children were the most senior in the school and some were now taller than she was. In a couple of month time, they would be starting their new adventure at secondary school where they would once again be the small fish in the pond. They could be a handful on occasion, prone to lots of chatter, silliness and the odd fight yet overall Miss Sunderland had them in fine control. She had been doing this since she was twenty-one and fresh out of University, just seven years prior. She herself would be moving on to pastures new accepting a teaching job elsewhere, embarking on a more senior role as a deputy head teacher.

With both herself and the kids ready to end the school year, Miss Sunderland had become more relaxed and lenient on Friday afternoons. They had completed all of their exams for the year, finished the school production of Olivia, Oliver Twist retold with the titular character being played by a girl, it had to be done that way, as the boys really were that rubbish at drama, the school's namesake would be ashamed. So from that moment on, as long as the children behaved during regular lessons over the week Friday afternoons would be spent in a lesson that she dubbed 'Golden time' where within reason the kids were free to do whatever they pleased.

Therefore, they did, mixtures of children sat on the thin blue carpet at the front of the classroom peacefully reading books whilst relaxing on bright rainbow coloured cushions. Five or so had acquired the white board and used it to play hangman. The little girl who was the hangman was constantly winning mainly due to spelling mistakes in the answers, the worst being 'The Gardeners of the galaxy'. A few girls were sat at their desks making bracelets from neon coloured beads and braiding each other's hair, the rest of the pupils were either playing board games or with action figures and in the far corner of the room four boys were playing cards and giggling.

The ringleader of these ten-year-old boys was also the shortest. A red headed freckled boy by the name of Jack, leader by virtue of being the best footballer in the year, as at that age that was all that was needed to become the alpha of a group. Beside him was a tall podgy kid named Josh with frog like eyes, there was also Luke with a face that when smiling made him resemble a chimpanzee, especially with the big ears. All three had the same haircut just with different colours, the gelled forward hair spiked into a quiff at the end. The last of the boys was Callum, with blonde curtains and big buckteeth, there was nothing predominantly naughty about them but they had a habit of getting into trouble for being cheeky and chatterboxes.

Today however they were about to be in the biggest trouble of their lives. Unusually quiet apart from the occasional loud giggles. Their young blonde teacher excused the giggling as it was not excessive and besides, she liked the fact the boys were enjoying themselves, assuming they were going through their football player trading cards. Half way through the lesson Miss Sunderland journeyed around her classroom taking an interest in her kid's activities, she could not help but smile seeing the children she had taught and nurtured for the last eleven months having so much fun and the aura of the room was of a chilled capacity.

That changed however as she got to the fabulous fours table, the boys still engrossed in their cards did not see Miss Sunderland approach them from behind, the first they knew of it was when she was so shocked and outraged, she nearly choked breathing in. Callum immediately burst into tears hiding his head in his folded arms, Josh and Luke went red in the face avoiding eye contact with anyone, as the rest of the class stared over they could see that Jack was white and trembling.

Miss Sunderland herself also started trembling as she could not believe what she was seeing, this was a first for her and she was not entirely sure how to deal with the situation but also did not want to make a scene, shout or disrupt her other children's afternoon. The situation made itself slightly easier when Jack bravely admitted that the cards were his. Nodding Miss Sunderland confiscated the cards and held them tightly to her chest guarding them. She then asked one of her most trusted girls, Molly, to go and ask for Miss McDonald to urgently come to the classroom and off she skipped blissfully unaware of the severity of the situation.

The end of the school day came and went. Josh, Luke and Callum had all been dismissed home with their disappointed parents after Miss Sunderland had informed them all what had transpired during the afternoon. It was a different scenario for Jack however, who sat impatiently petrified in the Head teacher's office. He was on a chair that was typically for use by adults. His legs were stretched outright because they were too short to bend at the knee over the edge of the purple cushioned chair, he tried to rest his arms on the wooden arms of the but the gap was too wide to be comfortable. The magnolia coloured wall was plain and boring and after reading the same poster for the tenth time, he focused on picking a scab on his knee. It was that or he would have to look at Miss McDonald. Her beak like nose pointed at him accusingly with her neck length black hair cut too straight, her most distinctive feature was the faint moustache that everyone knew was there but nobody dared to mention. Word on the playground was that she was a lesbian, Jack and the rest of the lads would often say.

"Eww she's a lesbian?" but each confided in each other that they didn't know what a lesbian was but pretended to be in the know to look cool.

Looks aside, she was a favourite amongst parents, despite looking hard she truly cared about the children in her school, was fair, and listened to everybody. The children liked her as well but there was always a fear about getting on her bad side.

Unfortunately for Jack that had happened today, yet she was not judgemental and told Jack that she was not angry, more disappointed and that she was sorry for having to get the police involved but it was protocol for such an incident. Sitting in the middle of the desk that separated Head teacher and pupil was the dreaded cards, which were now placed in a clear plastic sandwich bag on the police's advice. Staring up at both was the four of Spades yet instead of the spade symbol instead was a black permed woman in all her exposed glory, with long pointed red nails to go along with other pointed parts of the anatomy, lying provocatively on a sun lounger. Underneath the card was fifty-one other naked women from the 1970's. Miss McDonald could not help but feel for Jack as he sat there obviously ashamed and scared.

Down by the school office Miss Sunderland was sitting behind the pine desk the receptionists would occupy during the working day. She had already comforted Jacks mother and convinced her to wait at home for more news, she also had to sign for a delivery of exercise books. Typical, she started thinking, all those years at university, about to become a deputy head teacher, yet if she is sat behind, a receptionist's desk then people automatically assume she is one.

She used the rest of the time she spent waiting marking some of the children's books from the work they did in English that morning. She was marking one child's book report and underlined the word 'severed' in red, she had a little chuckle and wrote the correct spelling 'served' above it. The book was about a dog working in a fast food restaurant; she could not help but wonder how some of her children will survive the work increase at secondary school.

For a moment, she had completely forgotten that she was down by reception and what she was waiting for. When she marked books, she went into auto pilot mode so she may as well have been in her own classroom until she was interrupted as a large shadow emerged over the book she was marking. The eclipse was caused by the big, bald, black gentleman stood in front of her, he had not said a word instead he awaited recognition from Miss Sunderland in her own time. He stood there with his Identification waving in one hand, his other stroking his finely shaped, dark goatee. He stroked habitually almost showing impatience as the small blonde woman in front of him failed to notice his presence until a few moments passed. His eyes were a hard brown, intimidating but his face showed a coolness that made him seem easy to approach. Miss Sunderland noticed how wide his shoulders were and how his grey blazer struggled to go over them before she realised she had spent too long looking at him and not greeted him yet.

"Are, are you, sorry, you must be the detective we've been waiting for." She almost started to stutter on her words nervously as if she was the one that was about to be investigated.

"That's right I'm chief inspector Foreland, I specialize in the illegal use of erotica department here in the south east" His cool voice was deep yet soothing and calming, he however did notice the shakiness in the young women's green eyes. "Hey relax, I know you're worried about your student, as is the head, his parents and probably the young man himself, this is just a formality and it will all soon be done with."

If Miss Sunderland was honest he did manage to calm her, but relaxed she was not, his demeanour and voice made her leg twitch, she found herself attracted to this man who was at least twice her age. To distract herself from distasteful thoughts she shook his strong hand and led him down the corridor towards Miss McDonald's office desperately trying to say positive things about Jack to paint a picture of innocence about him. She finished by explaining that he is a good kid, cheeky but good, and that she did not think he realised what he had done wrong.

"I'm sure he is, look I was young once, and boys will be boys. My own son ten years ago got caught playing a game on the internet at school; you picked a girl, and then collected beer bottles and for every ten you collected she took an item of clothing off. He got caught and the same was said, however, that was a different time, he got off with a slap on the wrist, here and now, we have to investigate this, the same as every incident, just to make sure this kind of accident doesn't happen again."

"You seem to know a lot about this game." Miss Sunderland was walking in front of the detective and looked back to notice him staring at her rear end and became conscious of how tight her black trousers were. To her shock he did not stop, so she looked forward the rest of the short duration to the office trying to walk as unsexy as she could.

"Well I'd be lying if I said when I found out I didn't have a try at the game myself. This was before the ban remember, but I'd be damned if I could ever get her to even take her damn jacket off, those bottles moved far too fast for me" Miss Sunderland giggled but couldn't determine if he was joking around or genuinely annoyed at losing the game, thanks to his deep, soothing, London based voice.

They entered the office and to Jack it was as if the giant was after him, it suddenly dawned on him how much trouble he was in, even more so when he heard the word 'detective' and 'from the police'. He was stuck frozen in his chair caught in two minds whether to leg it for freedom or cry for his mother. Detective Foreland introduced himself to the school's head teacher and used his coolness to try to lull her into a safe sense of security, except Miss McDonald did not melt under his magic. Instead, she stood nearly toe to toe with him and for the first time someone matched his strength in a handshake that he had to flex his fingers after to get the blood back circulating in his hand.

"So in my department we don't have many cases involving such young children and since there is no parent present one of you two would have to sit in on this." The detective explained, and although he had taken both of the women to one side and explained that to them discreetly, Jack had overheard and immediately darted his eyes at his class teacher.

"Please don't leave me miss." He said softly and Miss Sunderland was suddenly overcome with pride and a maternal instinct. For he was one of the kids that she has had in her care Monday to Friday for nearly a whole school year. She sat next to and gripped his hand and Jack momentarily had colour come back to his freckled face. Miss McDonald left the office and was instructed to go and wait in the staff room and that she would have to be questioned after.

Jack's class teacher was true to her word and not once did she let go of the grip she had on her pupil's hand. The questioning started well enough, and Miss Sunderland was impressed with how well the detective did to calm the young boy. First came the necessities; name, address, parents and phone number and so on. Then Jack was asked to give a run through of the day's events leading up to his teacher discovering the cards, if he knew what he was doing was wrong, his motivation for bringing them to school. Detective Foreland listened tentatively, and was swirling a toothpick in his mouth which he placed there at the beginning of proceedings.

THWACK! Out of nowhere the detective's large arms slammed palms down on the head teacher's desk. Jack and Miss Sunderland jumped in unison and their hands held tighter.

"WHERE DID YOU GET THE CARDS FROM JACK? TELL ME OR THERE WILL BE SERIOUS TROUBLE." Miss Sunderland was outraged with this aggressive outburst yet she could not ignore the twitch in her leg again. Jack was upset, but managed to stay composed as he explained how he found them in his parents' house, discarded amongst junk. After the questioning of Jack and the two teachers was over, the boy's parents were summoned to pick up their son. Jacks mum argued with the Dad in front of the detective, Jack and he teachers about why the cards existed in the first place, he responded that they were a novelty gift from his teenage years. The detective took over and was satisfied that this was just a case of accidentally failing to dispose of the erotic material. Still Foreland gave the parents a dressing down and warned them that further repercussions could still come to fruition. They were left worried about what was in store for them in the future and what the neighbours would think of them.

Later that evening Detective Foreland dismounted a sweaty, quivering, naked Miss Sunderland, the size difference made it look like a tiger mounting a kitten. She laid there breathing heavily one arm rested on her forehead as the black muscled, middle-aged man already started to get dressed.

"What will happen to Jack and his family?" It was not the best pillow talk Foreland had heard, but the young teacher regretted taking this man to bed before asking and she needed to know now her animalistic tendencies had passed.

"Well" He let out a groan at struggling to pull his trousers up without standing, and then a sigh indicating his boredom. "It was agreed Jack would be given a two day suspension from school but that would not hinder his progression into secondary school, basically a warning to anyone else who ever finds erotic content. After questioning his parents, I believed that the cards were misplaced and forgotten when it came to the extinction of erotica, and it was a small amount so the worst they will get is a fine, with maybe a suspended sentence. It might seem harsh but it could have been worse, we need to make examples of these people to prevent future incidents."

The detective was now dressed and Miss Sunderland finally mustered the energy to move as he headed for the door.

"Are you going already?" she asked.

"I am indeed; I need to go home, wash, and see my family then another day at the office"

"Your son you mean?" She said with a ploy to try to find out if he had any more children.

"My wife and two sons." he said without shame, the young blonde teacher went two shades of red, one for anger and the other out of embarrassment, she had been used like a plaything and felt ashamed of herself. Suddenly aware she was naked she jumped up and wrapped herself in her duvet.

"You Bastard." She sobbed.

"Look, I'm committed to my job, I love it, but I am in a sexless marriage, and after all I am a man with needs, with the erotica act installed, I have to get an outlet somewhere." No matter how crude that statement was he still made it sound natural and slick, she asked him to leave without looking the bull in the face; he gathered the rest of his items, such as his watch and phone and headed for the bedroom door.

"One last thing" He looked back as if he just remembered something. "Do you have that Miss McDonalds number?" He quickly ducked and dived through the bedroom door as Miss Sunderland launched a lamp at him, the girl could throw hard for such a small creature. It smashed on the door as it closed behind the detective and she collapsed to the ground in tears.

CHAPTER 7

Holly was glad when she heard the clunk of the Bunkers front door close, it had meant her father had been true to her word and got her some help for the Saturday afternoon shift. She had explained how manic they had been the past two Saturdays yet had no explanation for why. She had expected him to refuse as he was notoriously tight fisted when it came to spending out on wages but the takings were up so much from the past two weekends he could justify employing another member of staff for a few hours.

Therefore, Chloe joined her behind the bar. A couple of months' shy of her twenty first birthday she was a few years younger than Holly. The girls got on but Holly was praying the trend of the last two weekends continued because as much as Holly liked Chloe if they had to work a graveyard shift together Holly was going to be prone to getting fed up of hearing about Chloe's three favourite topics. These being men, fashion and trashy reality TV. Often when they work together Holly goads her into revealing gossip about other members of staff or patrons just to stop her own boredom.

Chloe was taller and thinner than Holly, her hair often changed colour but now it was light brown with the tips dyed red, her hair was naturally curly but today was straightened and regardless of the colour it always shined enough you could almost see your reflection in it. Her face was narrow, making her lips look bigger and luscious, and while Holly was confident in her own ways, notably with her humour and banter. Chloe was much more confident physically. She often had all of the men eating out of the palm of her hand and always had the longest list behind the bar of drinks bought for her and today wearing black leggings and a white shirt undone showing a low cut pink top, if it was busy she would no doubt be bought a few more.

Holly herself had decided not to make too much of an effort, a minimal amount of make up wearing just jeans and a white t shirt, her busty chest made the shirt look tighter than it really was. Holly felt the need to tell Chloe why she opted for the more casual look explaining how rushed off her feet she has been lately that by the end of the shift she looked like crap anyway. As they set up the tills, they talked a bit more, catching up on Gossip.

"So how busy has it been really? I was shocked to see my name on the rota." Chloe said, she always came across loud even when she wasn't. To Holly it seemed when she spoke it was almost like every word was squealed at such a high pitch dogs the other side of town could hear her.

"It has been ridiculous" Holly answered, unloading glasses from the dishwasher "I was hop, skip and jumping either side of the bar all afternoon, the worst thing is I can't work out why! We've been getting all the regulars in early, on top of that we have the dinosaurs and their wives, and I've seen faces I haven't seen in months and people I've never seen before!"

"Well this week you will have to share the pick of the men with me." Chloe threw Holly a competitive frown before they both laughed and carried on their setting up routine; both turned their head as once again the thud of the heavy front door echoed around the almost empty pub. There were no prizes for guessing who were going to be the first people in the bar and Michael and Tom came trundling in, Michael headed straight to the bar motioning to Tom that he will get the beers in, Tom as usual for the past two weeks headed to the Gents. Holly had guessed that something suspicious was up with the two friends and she knew she stood more chance of getting a straight answer from Michael. She had known both of them a long time and knew that if Michael was involved in some sort of dodgy dealing he would morally collapse when confronted by her. Strong women had always intimidated him, and Holly was the strongest, independent one he knew.

It was to no avail as Chloe pounced at the chance to serve her first customer of the day, and get her first bit of attention. Holly rolled her eyes to the back of her head as Chloe put on the same performance she does for every male punter. She asked what they were having to drink, each of her hands grasping a beer pump suggestively. She pokes her head between the pumps with a slight pout and a flick of the hair, she dumbs her voice down making her seem more naïve, she asks how the customer is doing, in Michael's case how himself and Tara are getting on. He replied that he missed her and that a couple weeks ago, they had an argument about their long distance relationship, she awaits the return question of how she is, and as always, she replies.

"Oh, I'm ok" before adding, "I suppose." in her sweet innocent like voice, increasing the size of her pout. True to form as she handed Michael his order of one pint of lager and a cola for himself he offered her a drink "Aren't you sweet, that made me smile, I'll put it in the wood for later." She genuinely does have a nice smile; however, she was smiling because of her accomplished mission.

During Chloe's performance, Holly's eyes were fixated on the Gentleman's toilet door. She had no reason to complain about the sudden burst of busy Saturday afternoons, it was welcome during the quiet months, she just wanted an explanation as to why, plus there were so many factors that did not make sense to her. There was no reason for all the regulars to turn up let alone old faces crawling out of the woodwork and new people she had never seen before; there were no drink promotions, no sport on TV, no free pool or any competitions such as meat raffles. Then there was Michael and even more so, Tom. Tom had been the first person in the building the past three weeks, ever since his strange behaviour down the nightclub. He still kept somewhat distanced from Holly; he occasionally gave her the odd crude flirt, but no longer went out of his way to do so as he did before. He was also using the toilet an awful lot, more often than when people break the seal after a few drinks.

Her mind started all sorts of wild theories and accusations, the two prominent ones were that they found themselves involved in drugs, either using or dealing. She dismissed both of those, Michael was even too scared to smoke a cigarette let alone try anything else, and surely the odd mixture of clientele that were assembling each week couldn't all be after drugs. Moreover, it was the middle of the day. Usually the alleyways around the nightclubs on the seafront after dark was the place to get gear. Michael had seemed shaky and nervous a couple of weeks ago but settled down a bit last week and this week was back to normal. Holly though, put that down to him and Tara, he already said to Chloe about an argument he had had with his long-time girlfriend, and she knew Michael was the type to over worry about what was probably a petty fight.

Was Tom seriously ill? That was the next thought to rush to the front of Holly's head as she unconsciously rinsed out the same pint glass she picked up when she first stared at the toilet doors. He was in the gents a lot and for long periods. Everyone who turned up to the pub seemed to know him and came to talk to him. Were they all here to give him support and comfort?

"No" she said out loud, Tom would have confided in her, he came to her a few months ago worried he had a new mole or growth that had appeared on his neck. He was full of fear and distraught, sealing his own fact by searching symptoms on the internet. It was one of the only times Tom opened up emotionally to Holly and his anxiety was clear to see, she started to feel compassion for him. It turned out to be a chocolate chip stuck to him that fell from a cookie he was eating earlier in the day.

The whole time she was thinking, customers had been trickling in and patiently waiting to be served, as the patience wore thin for some punters they called out to get her attention, even Chloe told her to get her arse into gear as she was practically working the bar herself.

That was when Holly saw a scruffy chap talking to Michael, he looked unsavoury the kind of person Michael would not normally associate himself with. Michael grimaced after shaking the man's grubby hand. He had unkempt curly reddish hair and uneven stubble; his swamp green coat was long and unnecessary for the warm weather outside and the smell of stale beer and sweat lingered ever so slightly towards the bar. Michael, after a brief conversation pointed him in the direction of the gent's toilet, Michael noticed Holly had seen the whole exchange and he quickly and nervously pointed his eyes downwards staring into his pint. The sign of nerves and guilt gave Michael away to Holly, now she knew something dodgy was up.

"Watch the bar." She said to Chloe, ignoring the protest and enquiry for a reason. She wished now she was not wearing tight jeans as she chaffed darting from behind the bar area into the mainland's of the pub. She shot round the outside of the round bar like she was on an athletics track and power walked past the pool table and seating area making sure she got there before the shaggy dog in the green coat.

Her right arm was held across the door preventing entrance or exit and her left was pointed upwards towards the scruff.

"Don't even think about going in there" She directed through clenched teeth "either you can go and get a drink or piss off out of my Dad's pub." For a short girl she was feisty and the man looking down at her did not say a word, he just lifted his arms above his head in surrender and walked back towards the masses that had started to occupy the pub. She blasted Michael an accusing look, which he saw for a split second before he guiltily went back to studying his pint. Holly braced herself and took a deep breath before opening the toilet door.

CHAPTER 8

The stench of the men's toilet always suffocated Holly as she scrunched up her face feeling as if she was being poisoned. She, along with the other female members of staff were always perplexed that no matter how hard it was scrubbed clean the smell always remained. Even worse, the men did not seem to notice, mind or complain about the smell. She looked around at the urinals just to make sure there were no exposed men around, she noticed the tap was running on the sink and she turned it off, when she did, she could hear horrendous whistling, it was to no tune in particular, off key and sometimes just sounded like blowing air. It was unmistakably Tom.

The cheery whistling was soon drowned out by Holly thumping the only locked cubicle door, it then suddenly stopped as she called out.

"Tom I know you are in there, open up." Just as Holly could not mistake his whistle, Tom could not mistake Holly's angry voice. He stayed silent hoping, like a child, the trouble would go away.

The hunt had overtaken Holly; she was determined not to let her prey get away. She went to reach for her keys in her jeans pocket and locked the main entrance to the boy's toilets so there was no chance of interruption. Once again she turned her attention to the locked cubicle which she was a hundred percent sure Tom was behind. Tom however continued to ignore her warnings and after thumping the door again and breaking one of her nails trying to get to the lock undone, she dropped to her knees to scan through the gap left at the bottom of the door. Tom was not in there sat on the throne like she had expected. She was however certain he was in there hiding so she flipped and went flat on her back, it wasn't until her head was fully under the gap in the door she realised she didn't even check to see if the floor was clean, chances are there was hundreds of germs now partying on her back.

Now her head was under the door she could see she her suspicions of Tom were justified, first, she saw his legs dangling from the ceiling way above her, and then past his legs she could see his blue eyes staring down at her, he was perched in a gap where a ceiling tile had been removed. She was confused and angry yet she couldn't help but like the way the front left of his usually swept hair hung over his forehead, she thought it suited him, but all it took was for Tom to open his mouth and the anger was soon back at the forefront of her mind.

"How many years have I been trying to get you in these cubicles?" he asked, it was typical Tom. A crude flirt, the attention Holly had in truth missed these past few weeks but she did not find it appropriate at this current moment. "And here you are not only in the cubicle with me, but you're also flat on your back." He stared down at Holly's face, he saw how distressed she actually looked and he could tell he could not joke his way out of this one. His smile disappeared and he swung down to ground level, he had grown much more confident with climbing to and from the ceiling over the past few weeks, and helped the rest of Holly's body through the gap under the door much to her insistence not to and then against her pleas to be careful. The moment was made more awkward when Holly's chest got squashed part way under the door, blocking her progress. After a struggle she was through and Tom helped her to her feet and they were in close proximity, she was almost as tall as Tom which was not very tall but made an angry Holly that much more intimidating to him.

"I've been working on the pipes up there, it looked like you had a leak and…" he stopped his lie when Holly's frown said his name louder than her voice could do and as she sat on the toilet seat Tom looked down at his feet.

"We are locked in here Tom" she explained, "Tell me everything, why have you been distant? Why is my Dad's pub so busy? What have you got yourself and Michael into to? We have all the time in the world, I've text Chloe to let the men use the Ladies, said it was an emergency." She bombarded him with questions and Tom was shocked how calm she was talking, the anger subsided the moment she sat on the toilet seat, the distress had turned to exhaustion and she placed her arms around the back of her head. "Just start from the beginning Tom."

He still stood staring at his feet, Holly was one of the only people in the world that he hated to upset and he had upset her a fair few times in his life. Tom felt ashamed of himself for the first time since he embarked on his new business. He was worried what she would think of him, he was also surprised that she missed his attention; she always seemed so annoyed when he pestered her. He owed her one he decided and so he did what she had asked, he started at the beginning. From the moment he and Tom dug out that pond, their discovery, the fact that said discovery preoccupied his mind in the pub later that day, that in the nightclub he had been formulating a business plan. He described how the business worked and how much money him and Michael were making. He also told her that although he is breaking the law, morally he feels he is doing the men of Queensmouth a good service.

"I'm the Robin Hood of pornography… you could say Robin wood" He stood proud of that pun and was annoyed it was not used in front of the lads; Holly was still too far annoyed to even tolerate Tom's crude humour and stood up from the toilet seat prodding him with a finger firmly in the chest.

"You finish up your day in here." Holly poked harder "but it's the last time you're doing it, come and see me when my shift finishes this evening and we will discuss this further Tom, bring Michael and meet me down in the office." Tom was surprised at her lack of anger or disgust yet she did deliberately squash him behind the cubicle door as she left leaving him sandwiched.

Holly unlocked the toilets to find a cue of three men standing outside, they jolted upright in unison caught by surprise, two were regulars the other was only just eighteen, she knew that from checking his identification when the pimpled creature first attempted to buy a beer. All three tried to avoid eye contact with Holly, one of the regulars however accidentally did catch her judging gaze, a tall chap with white hair yet a dark beard stuttered trying to think up an excuse on the spot as to why he was waiting outside an out or order bathroom.

"Erm we are desperate" He lamely stated.

Holly looked them up and down in a way that revealed she knew their dirty little secret.

"I know you are." she sharply replied. She threw Michael the same look who, himself, was still standing nervously next to a vacant stool. Once she walked around and returned to work behind the bar she approached Michael and whispered to him "I know everything." Then she went on assist Chloe serving drinks. Michael then slumped onto the stool defeated and ashamed.

The afternoon carried on without any more disruption. Chloe had amassed a vast array of drinks from charming the men over the course of her shift, Holly herself had chucked her mind into her work so she did not have to think about the discovery she made back in the toilets. It also stopped the temptation to judge each customer whether they were here just for drinking or for a more perverted reason. Michael had returned to his uncertain, nervous state from weeks prior, he knew Holly had caught them out and although he was certain she would be too loyal to go to the authorities it confirmed his fears of how high the risk factor of their operation was. He also had doubts that customers would be too keen in further transactions now the cat was out of the bag; they would not want to risk their professional, social and family life for the sake of a quick thrill. Yet the punters kept going to visit Tom in the toilet like some sort of erotic Santa's grotto. Adam and Simon tried to put him at ease suggesting that Tom would have come up with a cover up for Holly's interruption at lunchtime. Kneecap being the smartest of the friends shared Michael's sentiments and suggested it might be for the best if Tom and Michael call it a day, dump the stuff they found and just enjoy the extra pocket money they made.

At the end of the afternoon Tom had time to join his brothers in arms at their table and was totally unfazed by the earlier proceedings, he sat calmly stretching his arms and legs in his chair as if he thoroughly had deserved it after a long day of strenuous work much to Michael's amazement. Adam was at the bar ordering bottles of beer for himself, Tom and Simon, a bright blue alchopop, minus the taunts, for kneecap and an orange juice for Michael. He always tried to walk back from the bar in flexing and strutting in a vain attempt to show off his muscles and as usual was wearing a tight t-shirt. Holly and Chloe were not impressed and mocked him privately to one another laughing at the way he tried to flaunt himself but they observed as he pranced away he just looked like a swaying monkey.

"So how did you do it?" It was as if Kneecap took the words out of Michael's mouth. He was glad to have an ally and someone on his wavelength he could rely on. "We all saw what happened with Hol' earlier, how did you manage to stop her from kicking out everyone in the pub there and then, or anyone catching on to the fact she found out?"

"It was quite simple" Tom said leaning forward.

"See what did I tell you?" Simon slapped Michael's chest with his long freckled arm smiling reassuringly.

"I told everyone she kicked off at me because she found out I shagged her eighteen-year-old sister." Tom had a way of looking proud of what he said even if it was the stupidest thing to have come out of his mouth this year.

"YOU IDIOT" Michael barked not holding back. "If she wasn't going to string us up already she will now, why do you not think?"

"What's happened?" Adams beady eyes looked confused at what he had missed whilst buying the drinks.

"Tom's had it away with Holly's little sister" Simon answered, Adams eyes almost doubled in size and Kneecap, Michael and even Tom looked at the lanky ginger man in disbelief that he didn't grasp why Tom had said what he said. The three of them silently debated who was going to lambast Simon first but before they had a chance Tom and Michael were summoned by Holly to follow her towards the back of the bar, the other three extended condolences and thanked them for the service they provided as the two partners in crime wearingly dragged their feet towards the doorway she was stood at. She was the angry mother sending her two boys to their bedrooms without supper.

She led them down a very short five-step staircase into the pubs cellar, which doubled up as a makeshift office. It was full of beer barrels, crates, bottles and pub snacks on one side yet on the other was a pine dining table with four chairs. There also contained a laptop in one of the corners, an old till and a safe. They both sat down on one side of the dining table, Tom for once felt as nervous as Michael as they watched Holly who was parading back and forth on the other side of the table with her hands clasped behind her back. The two of them awaited her wrath.

CHAPTER 9

Michael's hands were at full length, palms laid flat on the table, his rear end perched perfectly still in mid-air where the shock raised him before sending him stiff. His mouth was so wide not only could a train enter it but it also eclipsed his nose. Time seemed to have stopped for a brief moment whilst he comprehended what he was hearing, Holly was continuing to talk but Michael was not soaking up any of the information. He unfroze his blue eyed vacant stare to look at Tom sat beside him.

Tom's demeanour could not have been any more opposite to Michaels, he was leaning forward, chin resting on his fists, an unconscious grin formed on the left side of his mouth and he looked in awe. Tom had no idea his partner was studying him, but Michael was aware that Tom was listening intently, more than he had listened to anything in his life. If the teachers at their school had all been incarnations of Holly, Tom would not now be a decorator come porn dealer. It started with Holly lambasting them for being so stupid and if they knew the risk and how much trouble they could get in. She berated them for the secrecy and for dragging her father's pub into the mix without any consultation, and then she went calm and casually lifted one of her legs on to one of the two chairs on the opposite side of the table like a strong willed leader. Then she said the phrase that sent Michael into his state of shock.

"Boys, I'm impressed. I want in." Holly had always been someone who strived for more in life and always saw herself as becoming a woman who owned her own business; although she practically ran her Dad's boozer, she never felt it was hers. She saw herself ultimately opening a wine or cocktail bar in one of the nearer cities, before going on to managing and owning a club in London, the older she got the more like pipe dreams they were seeming. She had tried running her own boutiques and dabbled with mobile hairdressing but to no avail. But since running the Bunker she had shown great business acumen turning it in to a profitable place, now she was sat asking to be involved in an illegal operation, one that primarily involved dealing prohibited erotic content to men she saw as seedy and desperate. She was not condoning the activity but she did approve of the money and success.

"You know me guys" she continued, "I'm all about people having the right to do what they want." Michael and Tom groaned with Tom motioning to Michael talking mouth movements with his hand, both expecting her to launch into one of her equal rights speeches.

"Hey! You know the erotica Act did not just affect you men you know! Us woman divulged in some viewing time to." Holly paused, momentarily embarrassed.

"Carry on." Michael and Tom both said nodding and grinning.

"I mean" Holly stuttered over her words "not me per se, but some women have needs, and not just single ones. Michael, how hard has it been sexually between you and Tara" Tom looked at Michaels crotch at the word hard and Michael frowned back "you're in a long distance relationship yet can't do anything sensual because of the blocks."

"He gets her to eat a banana on Webcam." Tom chimed in and Holly looked at Michael appalled.

"No, I don't" He said directly into Tom's face before looking back at Holly "I don't! That was his idea."

"Anyway" Holly was satisfied she dug herself out of her hole, she knew them both well enough that passing the buck onto Michael would be the distraction needed to make them go off at a tangent and forget what Holly even said, sparing her blushes about having to admit to watching porn occasionally. Holly was no angel, although she still thought herself as being better than Tom, Michael and their clientele "About your business."

What happened next was akin to a small family business finally being noticed and invested in by an outside party. Michael suddenly felt like he was in a boardroom listening to potential expansion ideas, he then chuckled when Holly went on to use the word expansion.

She started with almost admiration for the whole operation, which pleased Tom. She also called him smart to take a risk and exploit a gap in the market that almost made Tom blush with flattery; it was not often he received compliments for his intelligence.

"Yes, but it's the black market." Michael interjected proving he was still feeling a little bit uneasy about the whole set up. Tom looked at him with contempt, dumbfounded by an uncharacteristic remark from Michael.

"Don't be so racist Michael" he turned back towards Holly and in doing so his face transformed from the surprised frown back to his smile, he pointed his pressed together index fingers at Holly "I don't know what came over him, we don't discriminate who we sell to, please continue." Holly and Michael both gave facial expressions of wondering if he was serious but both almost telepathically decided it was best to gloss over the whole statement and let Holly continue.

"To be honest Michael, I too am worried about ramifications of getting caught, and you know me, I've never broken the law"

"Apart from underage drinking" Michael started.

"I've seen you do the odd line of coke at parties in the past" Tom contributed to a list.

"Didn't you use to burn CD's of downloaded music then sell them to other pupils when we were at secondary school?" Michael added on his turn of the rally, Holly was not liking where this was going and her cheeks were redder than the dying roses Tom once bought her from a petrol station.

"What about that French boy you nearly slept with when you were twenty? You met him in the nightclub and it turned out he was fifteen" Tom was standing and pointing excitedly, revelling in Holly's roast.

"Enough!" The humiliation was too much to bottle up and it nearly made her explode. "What I mean is I'm careful and sensible… these days" and before the two men could add anymore sins to her growing list she decided to carry on speaking "and you're the same Mikey. So between us we could make sure the whole business is being ran sensibly and risk is kept to a minimum, leaving Tom to use his… charm and charisma to keep up the sales" She nearly said cockiness but changed it at the last minute. "And besides the money you guys are making is motivation enough for all of us to be careful, we all have our own attributes to bring to the table, remember I'm used to running this place. I believe between the three of us we can't fail" Michael once again found himself relaxing about the situation and felt more at ease with Holly involved, in fact the more she spoke the more he leaned back comfortably in his chair. By the time she finished her pitch Michael would be sat with his right leg up nesting on his left thigh, and his hands resting nicely on the back of his head.

It was clear Holly had plans and she laid them out as simplistically as she could, as so not to lose Tom's attention, she was worried she may have been too patronizing, even for him. She pointed out the potential for future expansion; they had a lock on a niche market that was popular, in demand, and as word got out, their empire, as Holly eloquently put it, would naturally grow. She also added that if this were to continue to succeed they would need more product in the not so distant future, she had an idea for starters, but it would take money up front and they could worry about it at another time in the near future.

She did concede however that with expansion would come greater risk, although the extra income from the pub being busy was welcome, the idea of illegal transactions taking place there was not.

"No more hanging out in toilet cubicles." Her next suggestion was for orders to be placed during the week either Michael or herself and they would then sort out appointments for the Saturday to receive their goods from Tom.

Tom made a suggestion that impressed Holly and Michael. He was dedicated to this scheme, there was no denying; he told Holly of the directory he had made of every erotic entertainment item they had. If they produced a catalogue of sorts making orders would be easier for everyone, and would be easy to keep track of who had what.

It was now becoming like a proper board meeting and ideas were floating around freely. Kneecap, Adam and Simon were bought up in discussion, Michael said how happier he felt with Holly joining the helm and agreed that with another intelligent, cool head like Kneecap involved then the increase in risk wouldn't be as significant. They concluded the meeting there and then; catalogues would be produced, Michael, Holly and now Kneecap would take orders and keep them logged. Kneecap again with Tom, as both were self-employed and more flexible with time, would collect payments during the week. Come Saturday customers would have an allotted time to come and collect their chosen porn, then Adam and Simon would become the lackeys that at the end of the week would pick up and ensure the loaned out content was safely and entirely returned. Holly and Michael later spoke alone that although they see Adam and Simon as mere flunkeys they would use the pretence of them being soldiers to allure them and not to offend Tom whose loyalty to them was admirable.

The last thing Holly questioned was whether any of the pornography had failed to be returned, Michael was certain it had not but Tom admitted one magazine had been lost.

"Don't worry though" he explained, "It was only one magazine, a rubbish one to, he was really sorry and paid a lot extra to make up for it." Michael muttered an expletive under his breath at Tom's confession and Holly had to explain the severity of this.

"That's not the point Tom, what if it got found and could be traced back to us? Then they found out we supplied it? We wouldn't stand a chance."

"She's right mate" Michael was once again relieved at this new support "Did you hear about that boy just down the road in Canterbury that found some sort of dodgy pictures? His parents were given a big fine and only narrowly avoided sentencing, we would automatically be punished much more, and they would throw the book at us."

The fact Tom remained silent and did not argue was enough to convince the other two that he admitted defeat on this occasion and was willing to comply and be more careful; Holly gulped as she said her next sentence, for once not sounding sure in herself.

"Unfortunately we might need to get our hands dirty if anything like this were to happen again" all three looked uneasy "Customers will need to know that failure to return the porn, loose lips, or anything of that nature, and they will be punished, you know with brute force?"

Awkwardness surrounded the cellar, stockroom, office combination and only the noise of a drip from a leaky pipe could be heard until Michael eventually broke the silence.

"So just like Al Capone in America, we're going to profit off of the prohibition of illegal merchandise and keep people in line, Holy shit, we're gangsters."

"Not prohibition my friend" Tom said with a proud smile on his face like he had just come up with a master plan "This is Pornhibition."

CHAPTER 10
Summer

The air conditioning was on the blink in the big open spaced office of the South East Kent Erotic entertainment department, it was making a loud, annoying buzzing noise. The three people situated within were all sweating. Rivers were meandering on foreheads and lakes appeared under armpits, yet sat at his tidied desk Detective Foreland still managed to look cool in his pure white shirt. Uncharacteristically though he undid the top button around his huge neck, it was that hot, yet he still made sure neither of the other two men saw him discretely undo it not wanting them to think he looked untidy. In reality, neither of them gave a toss. He leaned back in his swivel chair, rhythmically stroking his dark goatee before to typing on his computer freestyle rapping in Morse code.

Sat opposite Foreland directly under the faulty air conditioning unit was Detective Dent also known as the Dentist. A nickname he had begrudgingly learned to live with within the force. He tried unsuccessfully to get people to refer to him by other nicknames, but Dentinator and Dentosauraus never took off much to the Dentists disgust. What bothered him the most was that his nickname was only attributed to him because of his surname; he now reluctantly responds to the moniker and uses the pretence that he caught a killer because of dental records as a backstory for it. He was of an average height, which still meant he looked stunted when standing next to Foreland. He wore glasses to help with his poor eyesight and his brown hair was long on top and tidied round the sides. He used to sport a brown ponytail when working abroad in Thailand but was made to get rid of it when he returned to the United Kingdom. He worked best incognito, mainly because he did not look like a detective and used this point to protest wearing a suit but accepted it as protocol and today wore a ruby red shirt with a black tie, yet he drew the line at his footwear. He was more comfortable in Sandals than shoes, so he secretly changed into a pair of brown sandals as soon as he got into the office each day making sure his superiors did not notice, but to the Dentist this meant he managed to maintain a shred of rebellious behaviour. From time to time, he risks the ire of the other two detectives by resting his legs on his desk exposing his long hairy toes. One-day Foreland put on a surgical glove and bent back the Dentists big toe so much so that it made him screech like car brakes, he seldom let his feet get in Foreland's personal space again. Dent was also typing away on his laptop, yet he was pausing more frequently due to his disdain for the annoying air conditioning. He also stealthily attempted to out stretch one of his exposed feet to get more comfortable until a statuesque stare from Foreland and a shake of the head from the third man in the room made him pull it back behind the desk.

The last of the three men was Detective Samson. In his late fifties he was the oldest in the office, his beach ball stomach pressed inwards as he sat forward at his desk struggling to get his arms to reach his keyboard. He was just a fraction shorter that Detective Dent and on top of his head was short shaved hair where within was a constant battle between going grey and going bald to see who would win. Physically he was unfit yet his nickname of the tortoise also took on another meaning, he maybe the slowest when it comes to fitness but he always wins the race when it comes to solving crimes. His memory and observation skills made him a legend in the south east of England amongst fellow peers and the criminal world, and like the other two, he joined in the collaboration of keyboard thumping.

These three were all that was needed in the Erotic Entertainment department in the southeast of Kent and between them; they were clearing and solving cases of such nature quickly. They were so good in fact, the cases were becoming few and far between, yet they all sat typing up reports after cracking probably their most successful case yet. One that they were all integral to for its success.

Clank! The typing came to a sudden halt as the noise of what sounded like a hammer hitting metal echoed in the office. The sound however was that of Detective Dent's stapler smashing off the faulty air condition unit.

"This is why we need guns!" Detective Dent proclaimed pointing so furiously at the unit his hand was shaking and fingers white; Foreland sat back relaxed amused by the prospect of an incoming rant while Samson rolled his eyes and put his attention back to his computer monitor. "It's bad enough on the force we spend the majority of our time being verbally abused when we are out on the beat doing our jobs and yet when we do get off of the street to do some simple paperwork we have to put up with this fucking annoyance." The dentist ironically contributed more hot air to the room, he barely paused during his rant.

"But if air con is enough to drive you a draw a gun, what would you be like on the streets with criminals" Foreland chimed in with his cool demeanour and stirring the pot in an attempt to provoke his colleague for his own amusement.

"Well we will just have an office gun for such annoyances" In typical Dentist fashion he continued to argue although he knew he was about to lose.

"So the next time your hairy arsed foot annoys me I can simply blast it away." Foreland tugged at his tie with his victory almost cemented, Dent was about to speak before the voice of the veteran Samson intervened.

"Stop making things worse Foreland" He said in an authoritative tone and a slight chuckle. "Look Dent, it's driving us all mad! But saying you want to pump bullets into a cooling unit is just going to make us question your sanity, let's just finish off this paperwork and go grab a cold beer to celebrate, this has been our biggest bust yet."

The aforementioned case really was a big capture and all three played a part in its success. In this current climate, strip clubs were not only expensive but also illegal counting as a form of erotic entertainment, and four weeks ago, Detective Samson caught wind of a particular club in one of Kent's main cities through an informer he had acquired. He was a scrawny person with short, curly, blonde hair and constantly shaking. He was caught watching pornography in an illegal private cinema that was raided three months prior. Instead of turning him in, Samson managed to coerce him to spy and snitch on more erotic dealings he heard rumblings of around the local area. In return, Samson let him keep a single topless models newspaper cutting from a few years back for his own personal use, it was of a slim, tanned, blonde girl named Zoe, age twenty-one and contained her insights on the then current politics.

The scatter-brained man informed reluctantly in the back of Samson's car that before you even get inside the club you have to pass a scrutiny test, you were patted down and had your mobile phone confiscated on top of having to pay an admission fee. This strip club charged fifteen-pound cash just for entry, which was considered cheap. In the countries major cities in the country they can charge upwards to about one hundred pound. However, this club had other ways of making money. Just gaining entry to peep at the topless bar staff meant that the prices of drinks were inflated to insane amounts, with a two drink minimum policy. In addition, one of the dancers would routinely walk around the dark club with a silver bucket for tips to be collected, with a no coin rule as not to scratch the bucket. On top of that, there were private dances and extra sensual services, which both built up the income and profits of these underground establishments. The lucrative nature of these places, as well as the easiness of preying on the depravity of the countries males made it an obvious business for organised crime. London based gangsters run a lot of them from the Nation's capital extending along the south east coast of the country. It was also rumoured the Russians were involved with some of the bigger operations as well as trafficking girls from eastern Europe into the United Kingdom to further increase profit margins. Regardless of the financial burden, having to mingle with criminals and the risk of being caught by the police, these clubs tended to always be packed to the rafters.

With the location of the 'sexeasy' (police slang for a strip club or brothel, an obvious but not too clever play on the speakeasy's from America's prohibition) nailed down Samson consulted with the other two detectives on his task force about putting together a plan. Samson decided that Detective Foreland would be the one to infiltrate the club. The confiscation of electronics proved to be a big problem however, it meant no pictures could be taken inside and a wiretap was out of the question. So Foreland would have to go in alone and it wasn't long before he was sat comfortably on a leather sofa with a lingerie clad twenty-four-year-old brunette kneeling on his lap whispering into his ear. She was short and weighed next to nothing, her pink skirt barely passed her lower back butterfly tattoo and the glitter on her face bought attention to her brown eyes.

The young lady continued to grind away on Foreland oblivious to who her client really was, trying to tempt him into taking it further and earn a higher tip by providing additional services.

"Come on baby, don't be shy." She whispered delicately into Forelands ear with a Nordic accent. "we will be in our own room and we will both be left satisfied" she was certain he would be left satisfied and compared to some of the horror shows she had to please in her three months working there, this guy was a big catch, she was attracted to the dark, tall, handsome man that she was saddled on. Playing his part, the detective started to breathe more heavily and he slid his right hand onto her left thigh, his big thumb stroking it. She knew she had him in a hypnotic trance and now was the time to move in for the kill, build up a bit of trust. "My name is Erika, come on through to our private area, then if you have a good time you can come back and visit me again." This was a verbal click of the fingers and as she stood, she took her stallion by the hand, pulling him up from his seat she was in awe of how he towered over her, she dragged him through the curtain and into one of their private rooms for some private time. Foreland played his role perfectly and she had no idea that he was not shy or hesitant at all and that after he had had his fill, her life would be turned upside down.

Six in the morning the next day and Erika had just finished her shift. She wore sunglasses, same as every morning to hide not only her tiredness but to cover the shame she routinely felt a day after working. As she passed shop windows she looked at herself in her long cream coloured coat and noticed how well she blended in with the rest of the city life that buzzed by. For her journey home, she could pretend to be anything, come up with a uniquely different life story. Just like many of her early walks home she stopped at a coffee franchise to have a coffee and make small talk with commuters needing to get a kick-start before slaving away for the day.

Some days she would say she is a writer, others a secretary and her favourite, that she was training to become a fashion designer.

She settled down at a small red clothed table, she smiled at a middle-aged red headed woman who sat at a table beside her. Her voice was as pretentious as her pearly white dress suit. Yet she was still courteous in asking Erika about her career. Today Erika, part humouring and part confessional said that she sold drinks and her body to horny men. The posh woman spat her coffee back into her small cup, let out three loud hawking laughs, told Erika she was hilarious, and asked if she was really a comedian. Erika's little aside just made her feel worse about herself and made her think her life was one big joke.

Her feelings did not improve when she saw what was entering the busy coffee shop at that current moment. She could not believe it and put her head down hoping the man did not see or recognise her. She recognised him though, his giant black frame stood high above the rest of the humanoids and although he was out late the night before he looked fresh and clean for how early it was in the morning, wearing a tight black polo shirt and blue jeans.

"Erika, we need to talk." He sounded so calm and confident as if this was not psychotic, stalker like behaviour at all. Erika stood up, not entirely sure what her next move was, however not wanting to become a victim of what she thought could be a crazy stripper serial killer her instincts took over. As if a perfect cross was supplied to her she volleyed his crotch like an England centre forward, pushed through the customers, and made her way to the front of the store that seemed like part of her elaborate goal celebration, she took a deep breath as she exited the store, before attempting to run again.

"HELP, HELP, LET GO OF ME" Erika was caught off guard as two men linked one of her arms each and as a human daisy chain scurried her down an alleyway and into the back of a car. When the panic subsided, she saw her kidnappers were the old round figure of Detective Samson, and the hippy like attributes of Detective Dent. They introduced themselves as such and explained to her the situation and the severity of her crime and that she could not only help them but also help herself, they waited for Detective Foreland as Erika sobbed, the tears only increased as Foreland joined the car, and they set off towards the nearest police station.

It was left to the duo of detectives Samson and Dent to interview the terrified young woman and after eight hours, they had enough evidence from her to mount a case. It turned out this particular operation was being headed by a small time London Turkish firm who primarily dealt in supplying other gangs cocaine to sell before pouncing on an opportunity to open a strip club away from the capital giving them a chance to operate in a less competitive city. As Samson was the primary on this investigation it his case to pursue, make arrests and follow up on any trial that would surely take place, yet he was eternally grateful for both of his colleague's support.

Back in the here and now, the three men were giving their report a final read through with Samson reading it aloud, set to the tune of the buzzing coming from above them all. It seemed that they were finally heading towards a conclusion on their detail but keeping his mouth shut was something Detective Dent struggled to do and instinctively his mouth opened.

"And that's another thing" He started, going over the report kept him intact for a while but he could not help starting another office debate pointing an open palm at Foreland "Why is it every case seems to end up with baldy here getting his end away."

Much to the Dentists annoyance Foreland grinned and blew him a kiss before uttering.

"Jealous?"

"It's not that, well maybe it is, but you're a married man." Dent said trying to justify his jealousy.

"It was necessary for the case Dentist" Samson contributed adding the nickname relishing in toying with the Dentist's temperament.

"Well why couldn't it have been me… or you even, spread the wealth, we were paying for the service so it didn't matter who it was" Dent carried on in his pursuit.

"Foreland was best for the job, he is the most attractive and confident of the three of us, you saw how that Erika bird acted when she saw him the next morning in that café, imagine how much worse she would have been if she saw your freaky arse there, she would've kicked you a lot harder." Samson was telling the truth, he however left out the part where he would prefer to save Dent for the interviewing process because he was the strongest interviewer in the unit, because where was the fun in telling him that? "And as for me? My old boy hasn't worked in about twenty years" The three men all burst into laughter drowning out the hideous buzzing as the wise old man was pointing downwards at his crotch successfully dissolving an argument before it started.

The phone in the office started ringing and it was only heard when the laughter stopped. Foreland and Dent stared at each other like duelling cowboys in a standoff. They both went for their respective pistols but Foreland beat Dent in picking up the receiver first, meaning if a new case was on the other end of the phone it would belong to Foreland. He answered it while Dent ran around from his desk to his rival's and tried to pry the phone from Foreland's hands like a child. Foreland being much stronger and larger kept him at arm's length while Dent clawed away like a kitten. Foreland carried on his conversation composed and as he hung up Dent flopped to the floor in defeat exhausting himself in an already hot environment.

"Well, looks like I'm heading to the seaside," he said standing, using his giant left hand to iron out his shirt that Dent had ruffled in their scuffle. Samson looked at Foreland inquisitively prompting Foreland to carry on and explain. "To Queensmouth, four separate reports of erotic entertainment being discovered. That's a lot for such a small town; we don't even get that in some of the cities."

"You enjoy yourself, I'm sure it will only be a matter of time before you shag someone to do with the case down there". The Dentist said sarcastically sat on the ground looking upwards at his colleague.

"I always do, perks of the job" and with that Foreland left the office in a jovial manner hearing the faint echo of being called a bastard by Dent as the door closed behind him.

CHAPTER 11

In the last two months, Michael had become a changed man. Ever since Holly became a partner in his and Tom's shady business, he had grown much more confident. The whole operation was running smoothly and fears and reservations Michael once had were slowly subsiding. They were sensible and both he and Holly did well to keep Tom on a leash. The business was growing at a rapid pace, quicker than they had expected so all three were working hard to expand as quick as demand was reaching them.

On the plus side the financial benefits were astronomical, Holly juggled running two jobs in the same location, running a bar and a porn empire both from the same cellar. Tom had not picked up a paintbrush in weeks except to scratch his back in a spot he could not reach. All three were much better off and in fact, Michael was tempted to walk away from his job at the local leisure centre. He did not hate the job as such but there were certain aspects he would not miss; Wiping down sweat off gym equipment, the amount of flabby skin he saw on show when he was lifeguarding in the pool, setting up the trampolines and dealing with frustrated customers on reception who wanted to cancel their memberships. He also thought it was not a job befitting of someone who holds a degree in History, in fact he was hoping with more free time and extra money he would go on to do his masters.

He had actually written his letter of resignation but his experiences of the criminal underworld, and by that, he means all of the crime and gangster films he had watched over the years, reminded him of something: Money laundering. It was a credit once again to Holly coming on board and being another voice of logic and reason to discuss worries with. She too had started to consider this but she had yet to come up with an ideal way to do this. They mutually decided that until they have a concrete plan and an easy way to explain why they need to launder to Tom, that Michael should stay at his job and at least keep up with earning an honest living on the side.

Michael was happy going to work knowing he did not really need to be there and he was even happier as he parked up his black Vauxhall Corsa in the car park of Queensmouth train station. There was an obvious spring in his step after he slammed shut his car door and headed towards the train station. The day was set up perfectly with not a cloud in the sky and just a slight breeze in the air being enough to stop heatstroke. He paused turned and headed back to his car in a short sprint retrieving a big bright bunch of flowers; he held them outwards knowing the smell, although nice, would be enough to trigger his hay fever. He had been lucky so far this summer and the last thing he wanted was to become irritable now.

Standing behind the yellow line of the train platform, he waited, tapping his foot impatiently like a kid needing to go to the bathroom. Tara's train would be due any minute and he did not want to waste any of their summer together because before they both knew it she would be back at the same train station heading back north to University in a little over three months' time, and she was already later back than expected. Tara, when not studying, was working for the University in the Admin offices and they had offered her an extra month's work, which she was not in a position to turn down. When Michael had found out it had annoyed him and he thought she was the selfish one choosing money over him but looking back over what had happened the last month maybe it was for the best she wasn't around. On the other side, he could not help but wonder if his life would have taken this direction if she were around. He settled for the fact him and Tom still would have dug the pond and found the porn and Tom still would have embarked on this venture with or without him. Michael checked his freshly ironed black trousers to make sure his roll of twenty pound notes were still secure he was certain he had made the right choice, and in future Tara would not need to work extra months. Michael was now in a position to support her.

Along with his trousers he was wearing a salmon pink long sleeved shirt, with the collar done up at the neck which made him feel uncomfortable but he looked presentable, his hair was styled to perfection and he clean shaved the night before giving him the baby face which she found cute. He did not overdo it on the aftershave, instead leaving the aroma of the flowers to please his girlfriend.

The train crawled alongside the platform and Michael could see the silk blonde hair of his girl through the window grabbing her suitcase. He shuffled along the platform like a crab so he was positioned just outside the automatic doors and he would be the first thing her eyes saw. He held his arms out wide ready to embrace her as the doors swashed open. Michael almost jumped out of his skin when he saw standing in front of Tara a ridiculously short hideous troll like man, likely in his sixties.

"I don't swing that way." the troll rasped as he swatted Michael to one side climbing out of the train. Regaining composure Michael reached out a hand taking his girlfriend's purple suitcase as Tara giggled at Michael's mix up with the old man. He was not prepared for how heavy the suitcase was going to be as it pulled his arm to the ground like an anchor.

"Mind the gap." he said caringly as Tara skipped onto the platform stepping foot in her home town for the first time since Easter.

"The automated voice reminded me of that on the train Michael, I'm a Uni student, I do understand English" she replied in a teasing manner "now where is my hug? Or was it especially for that old man?"

Michael did not need a second invitation as he dropped the case and wrapped his arms around the girl he loved, then pulled back looking into her eyes before planting a soft kiss onto her as he placed his right hand on the back of her golden locks. He leaned back in for seconds but she dinked him on the nose with her index finger.

"Easy tiger, there is plenty of time for that, plus you'll squash those gorgeous flowers, for me I assume?" Michael almost forgetting he was holding the flowers handed them over, staring at her taking in all her majesty, he noticed the bright colours complimented her summer dress of horizontal stripes consisting of orange white and dark blue, it came out at the bottom like a flowery skirt, showing off her bronzed calves.

They were both talking about the last few months as if they had not communicated with each other, even though they spoke every day. They talked about the same things they had already spoke about; her studies and struggling with some of the boring modules on her course, his hatred of his job, her student friends, his drunken nights out, their respective families and so on. Yet in person, what they were saying seemed to mean more and both seemed engrossed, more caring and intimate.

Michael parked up the car and kissed Tara on the cheek saying he will only be a minute. He parked outside one of the arcades and she was puzzled by where he was going as he walked into one of the gift shops next door. When he returned, she was sat on her knees in her front seat peering out of the back window like an abandoned puppy but her eyes lit up when he returned. He had come back with a bag of candyfloss and two ice creams that instead of flakes had sticks of rock candy dipped in them. A creation both of them had come up with when they started seeing each other at college. She was touched by his thoughtfulness. When Michael sat back down in the driver's seat all he could see what the biggest smile in the world glowing from Tara's white teeth. He drove further along to a car park that led to a pathway that looked out at the calm sea, they leaned on the railings eating their ice creams and neither could deny the happiness that was felt between them. When they were together, they were one.

Later that evening after Michael had dropped off Tara at her parents' house he popped into the Bunker to meet with Holly and Tom. He was going to pick her up after she had spent time with her family and she was going to stay at his for the night but since lately Holly and Tom had spent most of their weeknights planning and working on the business, he thought it was only fair he contributed. In addition, he had something to tell them both, something he wanted Tom to know before the rest of the lads or even his own parents.

The pub cellar had not changed in aesthetics over the past two months, it was still dark and dingy, and the occasional drip could still be heard and not located. Yet it was clear this space under the pub was functioning as two separate entities, in one half you still had all of the usual public house supplies yet the other was becoming a pornographic factory and a business office. With the customer numbers steadily rising and demand increasing Holly sought out new ways to increase productivity. The first was to obtain a high definition photocopier to copy their existing supply of magazines into duplicates, DVD's were always the most popular option but there was still a market for the paper form.

"You can even take it to the toilet with you or hide it in a paper and read it on the bus," Tom said trying to explain to Holly how the discretion of the magazine still made it a viable option, an explanation that Holly rightfully grimaced at. The rules maintained the same, the magazine would have to be bought back to them but they never had to worry about running out of stock of popular issues, or have to be concerned if a magazine had to be destroyed due to damage. Secondly behind the table and chairs where the three entrepreneurs originally became partners was an office desk with a black computer propped on top. This served two purposes and both were important, firstly, Holly and Michael helped Tom convert his original database he created into electronic form in ways of a spreadsheet, it kept it neater and easier to update. Secondly was the DVD re-writer attached to it. Much like the magazines, the re-writer was used to produce more copies of their main source of income the DVD's. When a certain film had been copied the disc was placed behind the original in a plastic wallet keeping them all in order, this meant that under the desk was an open box of blank disc's ready to become of value, to the right of the desk was two more boxes of unopened discs.

Only one issue came up during this operation and that was what to do when the brewery came to do a delivery but that was solved in a simple way. On delivery day, no one was to go into the cellar other than Holly and everything liable was to be hidden, the men delivering the beer had no reason to question why a photocopier and computer would be in a pub cellar and naturally just assumed it was an office for stocktaking.

When Michael came down the few steps into the cellar Tom was sitting on a wooden bar stool he had taken from upstairs, stapling together pages from a magazine that had just been printed from the copier, in his black sport shorts and matching vest he was in full summer mode. Michael gave Tom credit, he had never worked so hard at anything in his life and it was almost soothing to see him find a purpose. Holly was sat at the table in the middle checking a list of who had paid and who still owed money. In front of her were ten tall stacks of bank notes ranging from fifties to tens, she reached under the table into a brown sack and pulled out another handful of notes, ticked some names of her register and counted an eleventh stack of five hundred pound. Holly had also taken a lot of pride in what she was doing and the more successful the three were the more committed she became. Michael thought it was also nice to see Holly making the most of her business acumen at last. She was not dressed as casual as Tom and had in fact started dressing in smarter business attire on a day to day basis. She was wearing a thin, sleeveless, red collared shirt with a thin gold locket hanging over the top of it, on the back of her chair was a blazer and she was wearing a black skirt with black expensive shoes. There was something about looking the real deal that appealed to Holly and made her feel successful.

Both were so into their respective tasks they Michael was unintentionally ignored when he greeted them a first and then a second time. A loud fake cough caught their attention yet he still was not greeted with the warmest of welcomes from Tom.

"Thought you were with the bird?" Holly turned and stabbed Tom with a pencil in the arm, not appreciating females being compared to feathered creatures. "Making up for lost time and that." Tom never even looked up from his magazine producing, he hated when Tara was in town because that meant he was no longer Michaels top priority.

"Yeah, I was but she has gone to visit her parents and sister before staying over tonight" Michael answered with not much enthusiasm.

"Nice" Tom's reply was quick but gave Michael a wink of approval and made suggestive mannerisms with his hands placing two of his fingers from his left into the circle he made with the thumb and index on his right.

Michael mumbled something with his hands in his pockets looking down at his brown shoes, both Tom and Holly stopped what they were doing and looked at him and urged him to say it again wanting to make sure they were not mistaken with what they had just heard.

"I said I'm going to ask Tara to marry me." He said relieved to finally get it out in the open, Tom shrugged acceptance and nodded before going back to retrieving pages from the photocopier and stapling together another batch. Holly on the other hand shot up. In some aspects, Holly was not a typical girly girl but in others she was, she loved a wedding. She flew towards Michael hugging him and bombarded him with questions like he was being interrogated.

"Ohmygod, ohmygod, ohmygod; How are you going to ask her? Do you think she will say yes? When are you going to do it?" and so on, there was no pause between questions to even answer. Michael wanted to take her batteries out "I need to go tell Chloe." she was heading towards the cellar steps when Michael grabbed her by the arm.

"Don't you dare, if you tell Chloe the whole pub will know, or she will put something on social media and Tara will find out!" Holly accepted this and calmed down not wanting to risk any potential ruin on Michael's magic moment. "I have it all planned out, we are going to play Mini golf next week, the one down the seafront where we had our first date, I have had a word with the owner and have given him the ring to place under the wooden bridge connecting two of the holes. I'm going to hit my ball in the water on purpose and when I retrieve it I will pick up the ring and already be on one knee and turn and ask her."

Holly was giddy clapping her hands faster than a humming bird's wings.

"It's perfect" and she hugged Michael again.

"Wait" Tom interrupted the moment looking up at Michael from over the top of a dirty magazine "You're going to knock it in to the water? You will lose!" Tom seemed genuinely confused by this whole concept "Why would you want to lose on purpose?"

"Oh shut up Tom." Holly came to Michaels defence as if he was her new pet.

"Hey!" Michael looked at Tom confidently "I thought my best man would be happy for me." Suddenly Tom rose and walked towards Michael. He was overwhelmed. He was proud. He was choked up. He hugged Michael as hard as he could then went and sat back down at his workstation.

"I think he approves." Holly said to Michael looking on proud at her boys. It was at that moment Kneecap burst through the door and tumbled down the couple of steps landing on one leg before standing upright and shaking his other leg in a sort of dance pretending the trip was deliberate. He was sweating making his thick black hair and eyebrows bushier, the dark black vest he wore revealed how good his physique naturally is, and he straightened up the right leg of his grey tracksuit bottoms, which somehow rose up, because of his fall.

"Either Tom is wearing that hideous aftershave again or something tragic has happened." Kneecap declared noticing how watered and red the three pairs of eyes that stood before him were, the statement was light-hearted but his tone was cautious just in case something tragic had occurred, but then he began to smile when he noticed the smiles on Tom, Michael's and Holly's faces. After a little encouragement from Holly, Michael explained the tears of happiness and Kneecap, flamboyant as ever, went for a hug that

Michael instinctively stepped back from, wagging his finger in kneecaps face and made a noise of concern. Kneecap looking down and remembering how sweaty he was paused mid hug attempt, and instead tiptoed and patted Michael on the head congratulating him.

"Thanks mate, I take it you have been to the gym," Michael said laughing, "You obviously didn't use up all of your energy the way you stumbled in here."

"I once read about that Indian bloke who held his arm in the air for like forty years, these guys never run out of energy" Tom added needlessly as he stood with his arms crossed and as usual Holly, Michael and Kneecap chose to ignore his ignorance.

"Yeah I went to the gym, but that's not why I'm all sweaty. After I did some of my rounds, collecting used merchandise as usual, and then I got to Malcolm's! He purchased LES201, one of our popular DVD's and one that hasn't been copied yet, and he is saying he has lost it"

"Which one is that?" Holly curiously asked; kneecap stuttered looking at Tom and Michael for help before attempting a response.

"Erm well, it's you see, a beautiful blonde lady police officer stumbles upon an equally attractive short, slim red headed lady criminal, they realise they love each....." Tom obviously fed up at Kneecaps lameness around Holly intervened.

"Some big titted blonde sort dressed as old bill has it away this this tiny red head criminal, it's good. Sorted."

Kneecap was actually appreciative of Tom's blunt interruption and they shared a glance before Holly replied, "Yeah guys, I meant, which one is Malcolm." The three men in the room chuckled at the misunderstanding while Holly was less than impressed. They described the man to her but because he was not a pub regular Holly was not familiar with him. Kneecap went on to explain that he did not believe Malcolm was telling the truth. Holly, like before when she first joined the operation, showed her ruthlessness.

"Well maybe it's time to send Adam and Simon round to Malcolm's and see what they can do, they're not on board to stand around like chimps, and tell them not to leave without the film or compensation." She ordered, it was the first time Kneecap had seen this sinister side and he shared a moment with Michael who was still not entirely comfortable with Holly's darker edge. Tom meanwhile had already gone back to making more magazines.

CHAPTER 12

The cushions on the White leather armchair were so deep and comfortable it almost swallowed Detective Foreland like Jonah in the Whale. With one leg rested on the other it made the right leg of his trousers rise revealing his white socks. His lips were pouted; carefully sipping the piping hot coffee he was given in a fancy blue and white mug. He waited patiently in the living room of the woman who had made contact with the police. She was just quickly using the bathroom so the detective surveyed his surroundings. The room was wallpapered in a marshmallow white and pink with a dark red carpet, a rug covered the middle of the room with diamond patterns consisting of greens, reds and blues. A picture on the wall caught the detective's attention. The landscape showed what Queensmouth was like in the late 1800's. This was Forelands first visit to the tip of the south east of England and from what he saw so far he thought he would have preferred how it looked then, with the painting showing a glistening light blue sea full of old fishing boats ready to embark on a day of work and a Victorian pier in its majesty. Foreland had heard the pier was destroyed by a great storm in the eighties.

The house he was in however he appreciated, it was well furnished and the husband and wife obviously were hard working and had a bit of money. There was a large flat screen television in the corner as well as all other sorts of modern technology sprawled across the living room. He would like to think the new games console under the TV meant the couple had children but the detective had learned to realise how many men his age wasted their lives playing fake adventures pretending to be something else.

The woman of the house appeared in front of him heading straight to the windows looking out the white netting as if to make sure the coast was clear and no one knew there was a detective in her living room. With his cup of coffee just in front of his face, he was not sure whether the steam came from his beverage or the voluptuous woman with her back to him. Her purple dress smoothly went round her slightly wide hips and dipped in like a valley at her buttocks. The dress finished around the thighs and bright white high heels propped up her tanned legs. Detective Foreland studied her light brown hair and raised an eyebrow in approval of the well-decorated bun it was placed in. When she turned to face Foreland he could see this woman spent a lot of time on her appearance, with the tanned face and make up a plenty she could almost be accused of wearing a mask, but at least it would be a pretty mask.

As the woman spoke all unsavoury thoughts left Forelands mind, he was above all, a detective first. He knew his conduct and the amount of woman he had bedded that were directly linked to his cases was high and unprofessional but he never pursued until he thought it appropriate; like the young teacher in Canterbury or necessary; like the prostitute on Detective Samson's case. The thirty something year old woman opened her mouth and started to speak softly he could sense worry and betrayal, and he used his soothing voice to console her.

"Look, Mrs. Hamilton, come and sit over here and just treat this as a friendly chat, you obviously had concerns to ring us, so think of me more as a counsellor to get things off your chest." Mrs Hamilton grinned her purple lips and sat, as directed by the detective's large hands, on the red leather sofa beside the armchair Foreland was sat in. She was sat leaning forward, her arms squarely in her lap attempting not to meet the detective's line of sight. They stayed like that for a moment, enough time for another sip for the detective until she decided to speak in her quiet high-pitched voice.

"I didn't mean to ring up; I was angry, scared and a little hurt" eventually she managed to look him in the eyes "I don't want to get my husband into trouble, I love him"

"You rang because it was the right thing to do Mrs. Hamilton, now show me what you have and then we can see how we can help your husband; he might be able to tell us where he got it from." He was a natural at giving the reassuring lies, then like a used car salesperson, he finished his pitch with his favourite line "Let's stop this from happening to anybody else."

Tears were just barely visible in Mrs. Hamilton's eyes but they were there and her smile widened reassured and thankful for the detectives help, she perched up for a split second again looking out of the window to her left still making sure there was no one there even though she knew no one could look in. She took just a couple of steps before getting on her knees and reaching under the rug that lay in the middle of the living room where she was hiding what she had phoned about. Foreland was getting a good view from behind and took time to appreciate her curves, beginning to imagine her on her knees in other situations.

"Here it is" Mrs Hamilton was now facing the detective on her knees mere inches from his lap with a brown envelope that she carefully placed down on his lap, she accidentally brushed his thigh and blushed with embarrassment before quickly returning to her seat on the sofa. Foreland did not notice her ever so discreetly shuffle to the furthest point of the sofa away from him. Instead, he took his thin reading glasses from his blazer pocket and put them on before opening the brown envelope, it was the size of a magazine but it bulged towards the bottom. Inside, to his guess was a magazine but it was a tight fit so instead he turned the envelope upside down letting a plastic DVD case slip out into his hands, the magazine then came out of the envelope easier. Both were of a pornographic nature. It shocked the wife how professional and composed Foreland was whilst closely inspecting the sexual content because even she got slightly aroused looking through the magazine when she first found it, it was natural. "I suppose you're used to seeing this kind of thing." She asked hoping for an explanation and to break the silence that emanated from his investigating, he did not offer an answer.

Upon inspecting every inch of the magazine and DVD he placed them both back into the envelope and rested it on the right arm of his seat, he ironed out his trousers with his hands and straightened his purple tie, he looked at Mrs Hamilton with one eyebrow cocked and his face showed contempt and disgust.

"I have to be honest with you, this doesn't look good." He tutted then looked the worried looking wife dead in the eyes. "Your husband will probably get into a lot of trouble for this." Almost as soon as he finished the sentence, Mrs. Hamilton detonated, bursting into tears. She sobbed so loud she did not hear Foreland try to console her. He attempted again this time with a louder "But" and as suddenly as the crying started, it stopped as her optimism took over and she was all ears for a way out of this predicament. Foreland returned to his calm manner as he explained "Both of these are copies, they were manufactured and the good condition of them makes me believe they were purchased recently, you said yourself you only discovered them a few days ago."

"So what are you trying to say?" Mrs Hamilton said trying to pry the detective into putting her out of her misery quickly.

"It means someone out there must have supplied this filth to your husband. Someone with access to brand new, pristine material, or the ability to manufacture." Foreland's detective skills were never in doubt, second only to his ability to seduce vulnerable woman, and his grin revealed how proud he was at deducing this. His voice held a slight tone of cockiness but it still maintained his smooth, comforting and convincing demeanour. "Supplying erotic material is much more severe than simply possessing, now if you can convince your husband to reveal to me how he got this stuff then I am sure we can arrange a pass for him for his cooperation and you two can carry on your lives peacefully."

Mrs. Hamilton held her hands together in rejoice, she seemed to be selectively hearing what the detective said to her, she seemed overjoyed and kept thanking the detective whilst trying to reach her arms around him to hug him, genuinely happy. She only stopped when the detective placed his branch like arms on her shoulders, not only did she go quiet but her body stopped flailing around. He removed the hands and they both gazed into each other's eyes, contemplating whether to move their lips towards one another, until the detective ruined the moment by standing and brushing down his trouser leg, reminding the conflicted wife that she had twenty-four hours to convince her husband to contact him or he will be back with a warrant. He saw himself out of the house and as he closed the door and entered onto the quiet street, he laughed and shook his head in disbelief.

"This is far too easy" he said to no one "Women are so stupid." Satisfied he had used his charm, police skills, and sexual tension to manipulate the woman into giving him a break in the case he walked the street to his car and drove back to his hotel thinking he deserves himself a nice dinner and glass of wine.

Less than twenty minutes later and Mrs. Hamilton was on her house phone to her husband and on the other end of the phone was Jack Hamilton. He pulled over to the side of the road in his shiny silver van, a yellow pencil behind his mixed black and grey short trimmed hair, his orange polo shirt was done up to the top button and his tan was a healthy shade of brown from working outside all day. As soon as he heard his name whine through the speaker he knew he had done something wrong or worse yet something was going to cost him money.

"What have you bought now?" he said playfully in his distinctive croaky voice. His face was visibly tired, his eyes red and his face wrinkled, yet he still looked handsome for a man in his mid-forties. As she began to speak the wrinkles increased, she explained how she discovered the pornography and in a moment of sheer panic called the authorities.

"Crap." He said under his breath pointing the phone away from his mouth so she could not hear. "I knew I should have hidden it better." Yet he was calm and sure he could smooth over and talk his way out of the situation, then the wrinkles on his face doubled as he showed more worry, she carried on with how the day went specifically informing the police. The sorrow in her voice was plain to hear but that did not stop Jack.

"YOU STUPID COW." He shouted, this time he did not direct the phone away from his mouth and he slammed his free right hand on the van steering wheel. "After everything I've done for you, all the blood, sweat and tears I've invested in making sure you live a life of luxury". Mrs. Hamilton was sobbing, apologising and talking at a fast pace forcing Jack to calm himself down and reassure his wife. She in turn reassured her husband as his head hung low with the phone held tightly to his ear and told him about the deal the detective offered, she gave him the detectives phone number and he jotted it down on the newspaper he had in the passenger seat of his van.

"Jack, do this and we can go on as if nothing ever happened"

"Ok, babe, I will sort this I promise"

"I love you"

"I love you to". Jack hung up and in the Hamilton household Mrs. Hamilton was smiling, crying and let out a deep breath of relief and was convinced everything was going to be fine. In Jack Hamilton's van, he stared into a streetlamp for a few minutes before staring at the detective's number on the newspaper before placing his mobile phone back to his ear as the ringing started.

Since coming off the phone Jack had spent some time sat in the warm darkness on a stone park bench, gnawing at his thumb nervously. Further along the path another bench was occupied by five teenagers, two boys and three girls all being loud. The girls were huddled up giggling on the bench whilst one of the boys egged the other on as he spun around drinking cheap nasty cider from a big blue plastic bottle. Jack was distracted so when he heard the voice coming from behind it slightly startled him, as did the hand placed on his shoulder.

"You'd think them kids would have something better to do with their time than that." Jack turned enthusiastically to greet the familiar sound of Michael's voice, yet he was visibly taken aback when he saw it was Tom's hand that was resting on his shoulder. Both were dressed smartly, Michael was in grey trousers with a black silk shirt tucked into them and a white tie, his shoes shined as much as the shirt while Tom was clad in Navy blue jeans, a light purple shirt, also tucked in with a silver blazer over his shoulders, Jack suddenly realised where they had come from.

"I hear congratulations are in order" Jack said, "I forgot the engagement party was tonight, otherwise I would have never asked kneecap to arrange a meeting tonight." Jack was apologetic and felt worse for the inconvenience.

"Hey, don't worry about that Jack; Kneecap explained the situation to us so we can't blame you for forgetting, and we're here aren't we, goes to show how much we value you." Michael replied supporting someone he had known a long time, a friend of his fathers.

"So what are we going to do about this situation?" Tom said one hand in his jeans pocket the other stroking his chin "It better be good, Michael left his fiancé and I left half a pint back at the pub." Tom said in jest, but Michael noticed Jack seemed unusually sheepish and looked threatened more than anything by Tom's normal jovial manner.

"Look lads, I know you know the situation I'm in so I thought I'd owe it to you to tell you face to face what I'm going to do." Jack looked both men in the eyes and showed true affection that Tom's body language changed from impatient to compassion "I love you guys, we all love you guys, the service you provide for us, you're heroes in a lot of our eyes. That's why I'm going to fall on my own sword, as Jeremy Bentham once said – 'It is the greatest good to the greatest number of people which is the measure of right and wrong.'"

Tom looked up at Michael for help understanding the meaning and value of what Jack just said.

"Erm" Michael thought looking for the simple way to explain it to Tom "he is saying the needs of the many outweigh the needs of the few"

"Like Spock?" Tom asked Michael beginning to comprehend

"Like Spock." Michael reassured before allowing Jack to finish.

"So I'll take any punishment that comes my way so you guys can carry on doing the good job you do."

Michael and Tom both looked stunned by the support and their gratitude overtook them; Tom kissed the top of Jacks head and rubbed his shoulder while Michael shook his hand appreciatively.

"We won't forget this." Tom said

"Whatever happens, we'll ensure you always have a place in our family and we will help you any way we can." Michael added, and he hugged the older Jack as he stood up. The man in the orange polo shirt left the two partners standing by the bench as he returned to his van. Michael turned to look at his friend by his side and addressed him.

"You know he seemed a bit off with you today Tom"

"How do you mean?"

"Almost intimidated by you, I'm also surprised he was willing to give himself in so easily"

"Well about that." Tom knew Michael was not going to like where this was going as Michael stared down at him. "Lately rumours have been going around about what happens to people who either don't pay, lose or fail to return the goods, or go to the police; bad things happen… but don't worry we've kept you out of it, they think Simon and Adam do the dirty work, and I step in if absolutely necessary." Michael in one foul swoop wiped his face with his palms and slumped.

"Why is it every time I think we're on the right path with this venture, you do something stupid? This is only going to end in tears, Holly will go ape shit when she finds out."

"Michael you worry, too much, come on, forget it, let's head back to your fiancé before she wonders where you are… oh and one more thing… It was

Holly's idea" after dropping that bombshell Tom jogged away from the park bench while Michael chased him.

   Michael gave chase after Tom trying to get him to repeat himself, Tom did not let up however and when they arrived back at the Bunker Tom disappeared into the swarm of party guests. Michael scanned the horizon to look for Tom or even Holly for verification but Tara's family members soon surrounded him, he tried to prove to be interested in what his fiancé's Aunt was saying to him and even remained polite when she patronizingly squeezed his cheek. His calmness was soon maintained when his wife to be grabbed his hand out of nowhere. Her new faux bob haircut glistened like a diamond, her Gold sequin dress made him want to protect his crown jewel, looking into her eyes, and seeing her smile back Michael had little care for whatever reputation Tom and Holly had garnered for them. All he cared about was what Tara would think of him, it worried him but when she softly kissed him on the lips, the ecstasy of the kiss took over and all cares were gone for the night.

CHAPTER 13

Simon leaned against a street sign on the corner where he had arranged to meet Adam. Being tall and gangly he looked more awkward than hip but in his mind he looked like a million pounds, he had new found respect amongst the men in the community and wanted to dress in a way that was befitting. After their first gig, collecting a lost DVD from some old sap called Malcolm, Holly had told him and Adam to dress how they wanted to be perceived when they go to enforce. Although they did the job well she told them when they go to make collections or threaten uncompliant customers they would be more likely to get cooperation if they looked the part. It did not take Adam and Simon long to decide that if they are technically gangsters then they should embrace it.

So for the first time since Holly gave them said advice Simon took part of his well earnt cash and invested in a black and white pin striped suit with a matching waistcoat that had a rose red tie and shirt combination hidden behind it, the left breast of the blazer pocket was also lined in red. He contemplated buying a matching hat but settled for a new haircut, his ginger hair had grown darker with length and was styled neatly on top with the sides shaved to almost nothing. He took out a thick cigar and lit it before coughing, he did not smoke but he took his image seriously. Through the freshly coughed out smoke he saw his associate Adam limping towards him and he could not believe his eyes.

Adam was wearing black, baggy jeans with the left trouser leg rolled up to his knee, the band of his yellow underwear was visible above his waist line and he was wearing a tight white vest which Simon would admit did show off his chiselled physique, he would also admit how idiotic he looked right now. A white baseball cap hid his brown curls with an American dollar sign shining on the front of it and fake gold chains surrounded his neck. He was now mere millimetres from Simon and any onlookers would not be blamed for thinking that the two were meeting to go to a fancy dress party. Simon stood upright from leaning on the road sign and pointed at Adam mockingly.

"Why are you dressed like that, are you off to a rap concert after?"

"We agreed in our texts we should dress like gangsters" Adam replied looking just as confused as Simon does.

"Yes. A Gangster, with an 'ER' not a gangsta with an 'A' I would have spelt it like that if I wanted you to come as a white Tupac. And stop holding your crutch!"

"So like a mafia guy?" Adam dropped his hands to his side, took off his cap, and rolled down his trouser leg feeling silly.

"Exactly"

"Well what stopped you? You in that black and white suit, if your lanky arse laid in the road the traffic would stop thinking you're a zebra crossing."

Both men had reached a stalemate in their abuse of each other and they knew that, they stood there for a couple of seconds before Simon said

"Shall we get a move on?" he removed his blazer and draped it over his arm.

They turned the corner they met on and walked along a road of Semi-detached houses, separated occasionally by a string of convenience shops and fast food restaurants. Simon was starting to sweat wearing a dark suit in the sun and was worried about how easily he burnt in the sun. He turned to look at Adam who as always was strutting and had tucked the fake jewellery under his white vest, now paranoid that he looked like an idiot.

"Does this not bother you?" Simon asked walking alongside his best friend

"Does what?" Adam looked up to meet his partners gaze.

"This false reputation we've garnered for ourselves, why can't we have had the role Kneecap has? You know, admin and taking orders, seems much less stressful and safer"

"To be honest Si, I quite like it, I like the fact people look at me like I'm going to smash their fucking face in."

"But what happens when we're really tested, and have to fight people, you'll be fine, you've got the muscle, but I'm not a fighter"

"Don't worry I'll protect you" said Adam winking and patting Simon on the arm. The two stopped at a metal garden gate connected to a short path that led to a white framed glass front door and it was not long after Adam knocked on the door a blurry figure approached through the glass and when the door opened the two enforcers were met by a familiar face. The house they had visited was that of long-time customer Jamie, he had actually gone to the same school as all of the lads and was always a face that was more than welcome. He stood roughly at five-foot-tall but was never taunted as a short arse, his size made him feistier and always had a reputation of a pit bull, yet more recently since settling down with a wife and two children, he filled outwards, as wide as his front door and his temperament improved. His yellow hair remained spikey like it had always been in their school days and his stubble only highlighted his double chin more.

"Afternoon Jay." Simon warmly greeted his old school friend.

"Ah Lads, I completely forgot." Jamie said full of sincerity and slapping his own forehead "You know how it goes, I just lost track, what's the damage?"

"Well we need back the two DVD's and an extra payment on each one for the week overdue" Simon said looking at Adam smiling suggesting surprise at how easy this was going.

"Okay mate, I'll be right back" and Jamie, leaving the front door open walked down his narrow alleyway and into a wooden door that led to the kitchen closing it behind him.

"This is going better than expected," Simon said to Adam "I don't know what I was worried about, tell you what I'll finish this off if you want to shoot over the bunker and get the drinks in ready."

"That sounds absolutely splendid, I will see you down there with a pint at the ready." and with that Adam set off through the metal gate and was soon out of Simon's sight. Simon was left waiting a couple more minutes, leaning on the garden brick wall watching his feet tap to no apparent beat in particular, then his feet pivoted towards the garden gate and he fled. He had started to run before he heard the crash through Jamie's kitchen. It was like a rhino chasing a gazelle, except the rhino had pace and a baseball bat. Simon ran for his life as a red faced Jamie chased through the front door and down the garden path following Simon who kept looking over his shoulder and was shocked how, even with his long legs and stride, this short maniac was keeping up with him, all the while swinging the bat aimlessly and shouting. In the panic Simon could only pick out certain phrases including;

"THIS IS MY PORN" and "YOU'RE NOT TAKING IT AWAY FROM ME LIKE THE GOVERNMENT DID". He was a man possessed. Simon decided to go into full sprint mode and recklessly ran across a busy road and only his long legs prevented him from being hit by a black cab, Jamie followed him into the road and that was when Simon heard the scream. Pausing, out of breath, he stood by the curb of the road to see Jamie lying in the road screaming. He bled from his forehead but the most distressing scene was his testicles being tangled up in the front wheel of a bicycle, beside the screaming Jamie was a cyclist in a lime green cycling jacket and tight shorts bleeding from his knee trying to console Jamie and asking passers-by to help. Simon with his hands resting breathless on his thighs was scared and exhausted; he contemplated going to help his one-time friend. Instead he remembered the front door to Jamie's house was left wide open so he headed back the way he had just sprinted but this time at a leisurely pace and went to obtain the DVD's. As he exited Jamie's house and went to meet Adam, the adrenaline was still pumping and he could not help but feel proud of himself, and that maybe he was cut out for this line of work.

CHAPTER 14

It had been a week since Tom, Michael and Holly had to sort out the incident with the detective who had been snooping around the operation, and only a couple of days since an altercation with a customer left him and his manhood crushed. Summer was approaching its end, which only proved to make Holly work up more of a sweat behind the bar. Football season had just started and live matches were once again being shown on the televisions scattered around the Bunker. When there was not football on the TV people were on the screen talking about football and when three in the afternoon hit the men in the pub would watch other men in suits watch and talk about other men playing football. This baffled Holly no end and as she was working behind the bar she was again greeted by the increasingly familiar sight of the back of men's heads, they even struggled to turn one hundred and eighty degrees to face the bar staff when ordering their drinks.

"Doesn't it make you laugh Chloe." Holly said not at all quietly but no one paid any attention other than her co-worker who looked over at her in her tight white trousers and light blue tube top, which complimented her summer tan. Her hair this time was curly and brown with blonde streaks. She wasn't wearing much make up other than pink lip gloss, she stared at Holly asking what was so funny without actually saying any words "I mean what would all these men say if instead of watching soaps we watched former soap stars sit around talking about what's happening in their program and we cheer without even watching the thing."

"I think it's fucking stupid." Chloe said standing tall and folding her arms and nodding in agreement and contempt. "All these stupid men stood here, would rather talk to each other and watch this crap instead of talking to two gorgeous girls and enjoying our charming personalities." Holly bit her bottom lip and stared down embarrassed at being called gorgeous, sure she thought she looked alright in her white and blue, square patterned shirt and she knew what she was doing by having the first few buttons undone around her chest. She even thought her hair being tied back tight looked nice, but gorgeous? She thought that was an exaggeration, she soon looked back up when Chloe carried on her rant and wagging her finger at the domed heads surrounding the bar. "Not one of these fuckers have bought me a drink today"

"No wonder we're both single aye?" Holly added, purposely winding up Chloe for her own enjoyment.

"Oh no" Chloe continued. "I'm sure I could snag any of these bastards if I wanted to, but they don't deserve it, none of them! Men are easy to figure out all they care about is Sex and football, bastards the lot of them"

"Ok Chloe" Holly sniggered and was enjoying Chloe's indiscrete tirade. "Look I'm going downstairs to take a break; can you cope for a bit?"

"Of course I can babe, take as long as you want." and with Chloe's assurance that she could cope Holly silently said thanks by moving her lips and trotted off into her cellar and business hub. She could hear Chloe in the background approach one of the few women in the pub and ask if she had read about what was going to happen in next week's soaps, Holly had to smile and sigh simultaneously,

"Maybe some women are easy to figure out to." She uttered giggling. With the door to the cellar locked Holly sat at her desk and opened her laptop and a spreadsheet containing all sorts of lists and financial figures popped up on the screen, it only made sense to Holly, Michael and Kneecap. Tom was insistent on sticking to his own system of logging the merchandise in hand written form and Adam and Simon had never even seen it before. She opened a bottle of orange juice that was by her side and once she was refreshed she studied the spreadsheet and in particular one big number at the bottom, which caused a grin so big it showed how white her teeth were.

"Chloe was right about one thing, men do love football and sex, and boy are they willing to spend a lot of money for it".

Holly sat for a while crunching numbers and the glow from her laptop made her face a pale blue making her look like she had been defrosted from the ice age. She jumped as the lock to the cellar turned and Tom barged through the door and jumped down the few steps jovial and clicking his heels together in mid-air. The only person other than Holly, Tom and Michael that had a key was Holly's father but he had not been to the pub in months' content with how much money Holly was making; he let her have complete control. Still there was a split second of fear in Holly's mind that it could be anyone walking in. Tom patted the top of the laptop annoying Holly who pulled it in towards her, Tom noting her aggravation removed his hands from the laptop and instead sat the opposite end of the wooden table facing Holly. He placed his feet on the table and leaned his head back into his hands; he and Holly made eye contact both with a smile, before Holly bashfully turned away her head pretending to fixate on the laptop. Tom looked happy and cheeky and it had nothing to do with the drink, he had spent the afternoon on cola, his gaze was beginning to make Holly feel embarrassed and she did not know why so she chose to break the ice.

"Come on then Tom, why are you so happy?"

"Well" Tom cracked his fingers out in front of himself "I may have just won myself a bit of money on the football this afternoon, turned a tenner into two hundred big ones."

Holly had to laugh.

"Tom we're running a business that is making us thousands and you are happy winning a couple of hundred"

"It's the thrill of the chase" Tom sat forward offended "besides it's because of you"

"Oh and why is that" Holly curiously asked.

"You're my lady luck, and that's why I'm going to marry you one day."

"Don't make me laugh Thomas; you have been saying that for ten years, the closest you'll get is now, as business partners." Holly blew Tom a mocking kiss that she regretted as soon as she did it thinking it was a bit mean but she was genuinely confused at how to handle Tom's flirting today for some odd reason, usually she could handle it. She figured it was due to working too hard and being tired. She threw him a bone "besides if you did manage to win me over one day, what happens then? Once the thrill of the chase has gone."

"You are the thrill, you're my holy grail." there was no smile or hint of humorous banter in Tom's voice and he gulped, completely shocked at what he just said, likewise Holly let out a silent gasp and for a moment they were the only two people in the world as they stared at each other. Tom felt ashamed of himself and Holly saw for once the real emotions hidden under Tom's armour of sarcasm. Tom shuffled awkwardly in his chair no longer relaxed and Holly decided to take the lead and put an end to Tom's pain.

"Anyway I'm glad you came down after the football." this time Holly gulped but with that, she put on her barmaid act with the false smile and charm, using it as her own armour. "I had to discuss business with you. Me and Michael discussed some things at length yesterday and I said to him I'd talk to you seeing as he is with the other half today, and ironically you gambling is going to help us."

"You have always told me gambling is a mugs game" the normal Tom was back in the room ready for a confrontation "and now it's going to help?"

Holly smiled that she had managed to ease Tom's discomfort and went on to explain the concept of money laundering to the founder of their company. To her own admission she was shocked by how clued up Tom was on the situation but as Tom pointed out, when the only films you watch are gangster films you tend to pick up on these things. She said that gambling large sums of money on certain bets could be a possible way to do this but wish she had not when Tom had a suggestion.

"Or I could turn thousands into millions with one bet, we pick ten matches, it's alright some of the blokes upstairs will help me choose." Holly found it cute how excited Tom was as he words spat like gunfire and his hands waved like fireworks. "As I say ten matches, and all we need is both teams to score in both of them, we can start next Saturday." Tom was bouncing and while Holly admired his enthusiasm, she had to bring him back down a peg.

"Well as I said me and Michael will sort this." The familiar sound of the lock turning interrupted Holly as Michael, with his ears burning entered into their headquarters. He was wearing red skinny trousers with a denim shirt done up to the Adams apple "Speak of the devil" Holly greeted Michael with a plea for support as he looked on curiously.

"Someone looks happy," Michael, said nodding at Tom.

"And you look tired" Tom replied with a nod of his own "Did she tire you out?" Michael chose to ignore Tom's taunts but his grin, upheld head and swagger over to the table was a result of spending the morning in the bed of his fiancé.

"I was just explaining to Tom about the money situation," Holly said looking over her shoulder and updating Michael on proceedings.

"And you're done already?" Michael asked sarcastically and Holly nodded yes in kind. "And you didn't even have to use any pictures to explain it to him" They did the same again.

"Pictures?" Tom mumbled not understanding the mockery, Michael was happily embracing being able to get one over on Tom, it was a rarity but he felt unstoppable at this current moment.

"Did you explain to him about the other thing?" Michael asked Holly

"No" she answered, "I thought it best to wait for you", Michael walked around the table to beside Tom, pulled his feet off the other chair, and sat next to his friend, his body faced Tom and he rested his right arm on the head of the seat.

"What's all this about?" Tom quizzed.

"Well you know we have been discussing expansion for quite a while?" Holly reminded Tom as he searched his head for the specific memories and made a grumble of acknowledgement once he remembered. "If we want to start selling on a wider scale we need a more practical way to produce the goods, we also need much more variety." Holly emphasised those last three words by speaking slowly, when Michael took over.

"Kneecap has heard rumblings of someone up north with a private collection, he has been boasting about evading police apparently and if the rumours are true he has a giant hard drive full of downloaded pornography, with a highly diverse… lots of different genres to cater to everybody"

"But we already fulfil everyone's requests with what we have got" Tom argued, just for the sheer fact of arguing and the tiny gripe of other people telling him how to run his business. He was in his familiar stance of sitting with his legs wide open and his arms folded.

"But" Michael paused for a second contemplating the best way to explain this "if we expand further across the country, maybe even nationally we are going to need to be prepared for every kind of erotic request, some of it might be strange, some unique and some downright disgusting, but as it stands we are not diverse enough. Hell we don't even have anything for the gay community"

"We haven't had any call for gay porn" Tom accurately replied not knowing the full picture. Holly and Michael looked at each other like parents preparing to tell their child their pet dog had to go to doggy heaven.

"well" they said in unison, exaggerating the word, as Holly then took the lead "we have had requests from a few people actually. Some you know really well."

"Don't" Michael loudly whispered next to Holly but she looked at him in a way that suggested that it was time Tom knew the truth and he stepped back conceding.

"Tom" Holly said kneeling in front of her friend and placing a hand on his knew "Adam is gay".

"What?" Tom hysterically giggled, "Do you not know, how many woman this guy has banged? I've literally witnessed it first-hand a few times."

"Tom, ever heard of overcompensation? He has confided in us, all of us, Simon already knew and kept it quiet. His main worry was how you would react; he can't risk losing you as a friend."

Tom's laughter stopped and a blank expression took over his face, he looked away from Holly and up at Michael and he knew instantly that it was true, the blank canvas turned to a face of anger and he as he jumped to his feet he threw the chair he was sitting on to one side. He thudded his way towards the door never looking anywhere but straight ahead before leaving the cellar and slamming the door shut behind.

"I warned you." Michael said, stood with his hands in his pockets and looking at a still kneeling Holly.

"I can't believe it!" Holly looked shocked "in this day and age, to have that reaction to someone being gay, even worse, one of his best friends being gay, it's disgusting behaviour! I know what Tom is like but I thought he was better than this".

Michael started laughing. Laughing so loud he started bending at the knees and with his hands still stuck in his pockets his looked like a dolphin dancing. Tears were visible from his eyes and Holly looked on with a newfound anger that she could not contain.

"What the fuck is wrong with the two of you! Do you seriously think this is funny?" she carried on her diatribe but it soon turned to white noise for Michael and he waved his hand in front of her as she pointed at him and he composed his laughter and straightened his knees.

"You have it all wrong." Michael still spoke with a giggle, and it was now Holly's turn to look baffled and she let him carry on "Tom did storm off because Adam is gay, but it wasn't because he is homophobic, Tom stormed off because he had a hundred-pound bet with me that it would be Simon who would be gay." Michael could not handle it anymore and completely flopped to the floor in a fit of laughter, Holly was confused but also relieved that Tom was not some monster, he did not care about sexual labels and that impressed her but she realised she would have to get used to the unique way his mind works.

CHAPTER 15

Everything in the hotel room was plain and neat, the furniture; cupboards, desks, the bed frame were all pine. The carpet and curtains were burgundy and the walls covered in a harmless light purple. Detective Foreland was getting fed up of the sight of this room, in fact he was getting fed of being in Queensmouth in general. In the couple of weeks he had been down on the coast, he had one lead, but the man, Jack Hamilton, turned himself in and took full responsibility for the crimes. Foreland knew that was bullshit but there was nothing else he could do. He would have gone back to the city if it were not for another magazine discovered under a disused railway bridge, it had the same qualities as the ones he had inspected at Mr and Mrs Hamilton's house, again it was not an original copy, it had been manufactured and had not been abandoned for long. Nevertheless, that was all he had, not enough rope to hang on to and he was beginning to become disillusioned.

He sat upright in the double bed; white sheets covering him from the waist down, his bare burly chest had a few black hairs curled on it. He stared at his neatly folded black suit and white shirt on the dresser wondering if it was even worth going out and trying again, to find any connection to his new evidence, he pulled on the bed headboard with his long arms and stretched when his phone rang. To his left was his mobile phone, charging on the typically pine bed side counter, he reached over his own body with his right arm and answered in his trademark calm voice, even if it was first thing in the morning. After conversing for a couple of minutes the gleam was back in his eye and his face became eager and cocky. He said goodbye, placed the phone back on the cabinet, and had one more big stretch before rolling onto his right and slapping the bundle sleeping under the sheets next to him.

"Come on get up." Foreland said as a mop of dark black emerged from under the sheets, hair all dishevelled before a young, pale face popped up with mole eyes, dazed and still half-asleep. She mumbled as she got her bearings. "Time for you to go, I have work to do."

He could not remember the girls name, just that she working in the hotel's restaurant last night, was nineteen years of age and studies photography at the nearest university. At the time, her hair was straightened, black and shiny; both ears were covered in piercings along with her nose, bottom lip and as he went on to find out, both nipples. She was not much of a conversationalist but she listened and had a bundle of sarcastic responses to anecdotes. As he departed the bar the previous night he had told her to come up to his room when her shift was finished and low and behold at eleven p.m. he had a knock on his door, she didn't need much convincing in detective Forelands defence. It rarely ever did; it was just another one to add to his tally. He had joked with Dent and Samson in the office before about when he retires what will be higher the amount of women he had bedded or cases he had solved to which Samson replied.

"Fuck off Foreland, you will never retire from shagging."

Foreland watched his young conquest's behind as she climbed out of bed without saying a word, she was shorter than he remembered and her jet black hair went half way down her back and it seemed strange for a girl so slim to have such a wide arse, which jiggled as she pulled on a small black thong. She proceeded to pull up black leggings and slip on her purple uniform over her head, picked up her heels and walked out of the hotel room without looking back. Foreland respected that, no hassle, no questioning of whether they would see each other again, it was no strings. Just the way he liked it. The detective was eager to jump out of bed, shower and get looking sharp but before he did anything else he text his wife a soppy message along the lines of missing her and the kids. He placed the phone down and leapt out of bed beginning to prepare for his big hunt and catching his prey.

Only an hour later and the wide shoulders of the detective strutted in rhythm to the sound of his black shoes clomping along a corridor in Queensmouth hospital. He knew the patient he had come to see did not have the ability to go anywhere but Foreland was anxious to make up for lost time and get on the trail of, what he was almost certain, the person manufacturing and distributing erotic entertainment.

A woman on reception pointed him in the right direction and after travelling down the long corridor, he entered onto a ward. He could not help but let his eyes wander towards some of the more fetching nurses in their blue uniforms, others however, he diverted his eyes and sneered as they resembled the fat, evil matrons you used to see in films from the sixties and seventies. Eventually he came to that of a private room, number three, the one he was told to head to by reception. He knocked and opened the door without waiting for a reply, making himself aware of how keen he was. What was waiting on the other side of that door was pain and torment, enough to make even the toughest man wince and cringe.

With his back flat on the bed and his blonde spiky hair rested on a pillow the short frame of a man named Jamie laid in agony. Both his legs hoisted upright and a cast surrounded his crotch and buttocks. He screamed as he moved his head to look at the detective and even through the pain, there was an ambience of relief over Jamie's face.

"Mr Brown." Foreland greeted Jamie offering a handshake, which the crippled Jamie accepted in kind. Even the grip from Foreland's hand as they shook caused him pain.

"Call me Jamie." the patient said through closed gritted teeth.

"I read your doctor's report Jamie" The detective rested his left elbow on his right arm and went for his trademark goatee stroke "and I got to admit you must be one tough motherfucker, I wouldn't wish this pain on anybody. So are you going to be the one to finally help me nail this bastard running around making and selling pornography?"

"Bastard?" Although it hurt, Jamie had to laugh, "You really don't know much do you. This is a whole operation, there is a whole team running things around here, and not just local either, they are selling countywide."

"Interesting" Foreland tried to conceal how pissed off he was that this case was getting the better of him. A detective of his calibre should be doing better than this.

"And trust me, I'm no grass, but my meat and two veg are now bangers and mash. Someone has to pay" Jamie managed to lean forward and point at the detective "So what I'm going to do is give you enough information to go off on and at least get the ones responsible for my injury. If you figure out the rest from what I give you then so be it."

Jamie stuck to his morals to a certain extent and as he gave an account of the day his injury happened and how the business worked, he made sure he did not implicate Michael, Tom and Holly. He didn't blame them for his injury and never dealt with them in the day-to-day operations he still considered them local heroes for the service they provide and part of Jamie hoped that long may it continue. However, his energy for revenge was focused on Adam, Simon and to a lesser extent Kneecap. He gave descriptions of all three.

"The man you want to see is an Indian chap called Kneecap, his real name is Nadeem Patel, he takes the majority of orders, get to him and you can get to Adam and Simon."

Foreland wasted little time in leaving Jamie to recover in his hospital bed and within minutes, he was out on the street ready to graft and find any of these three men and put this case to bed.

CHAPTER 16

Michael was about to live one of the moments he had feared the most. He stood waiting in the darkness of a long alleyway. The alley was the same length of Queensmouth's seafronts strip; behind the arcades, fast food shops, gift shops and pubs and clubs. Many of these outlets had back doors leading onto the alley and bouncers had chucked many people on their backside after being kicked out of establishments. However, it was the middle of the week and summer was dying so the alley was a no man's land. Michael waited centrally along the dark back passage, only three lamp posts occupied the long lane so seeing into the distance either left or right proved futile at this time of night and although he was hidden and the heat still persisted Michael was wearing a long cream coloured mac with the collar up and held round his eyes.

This was the last thing Michael wanted to do as feet crunching and scraping along the concrete floor gradually got louder coming from the distance. Michael occasionally bent at the knees as his nerves hit him with wrenches round the back of his legs, as little as he wanted to be waiting out back here he knew he was the only one who could meet this customer for the safety of himself, his friends and the whole business. When Michael focused, he could see a figure wobbling towards him on the cracked pavement.

The customer Michael was preparing to meet was well known to him but the customer knew nothing of whom he was meeting. A work colleague had placed the order on his behalf, the colleague made sure to note to Kneecap that the person who wanted to place the order was paranoid about his wife or son finding out so he had wanted the order placed discretely. Of course, Kneecap being efficient as always made sure that the man placing the order vouched for the customer. He did in kind with a picture and money up front, that was when the alarm bells rang in Kneecaps mind and within mere minutes, he had managed to get hold of Michael and told him about the customer, what he wanted, the planned pick up time and destination. Kneecap to his credit offered to do the drop off, noting it would be less awkward for him and the wise choice especially when Tom, Adam or Simon were the other options for giving an explanation. But Michael valiantly told Kneecap he will do it himself, it was his and Tom's company so he should be the one responsible.

As the figure got closer, it became less of a silhouette and more visible to Michael. Coming towards him was a man of similar height in blue jeans and a black rocker style leather Jacket that couldn't get done up over the man's stomach and was hence only partially done up. He shuffled rather than walked and even in the dark, the bald spot shined when walking under the lampposts like a lighthouse beacon. Like Michael the jackets collar held up high in a hope to hide his face but Michael knew with certainty who was waddling towards him. Likewise, as the figure looked up into the spotlight above Michael, he to, was not fooled as he approached Michael. Startled he decided to walk straight past without making eye contact and in an unconvincing Scottish accent muttered.

"Evening Sir."

The man breezed past Michael who in turn reluctantly sighed out loud and conceded he knew who it was.

"Dad. I know it's you." Caught out Michaels father stopped and slowly walked back towards his son.

"Oh Michael, I didn't recognise you there" His father said slapping Michael's shoulder "I was just out for a midnight walk."

"Dad."

"And then I saw some little pensioner lady get mugged and I chased the mugger down this alleyway but I think I lost…"

"Dad, I know why you are here" Michael interrupted the nonsense whilst his dad's nostrils flared and his face reddened "I'm not judging you, there's no need to be embarrassed."

"Oh that's where you're wrong Michael." That was when Michael first realised his Dad was not humiliated but instead angry. "Yeah I wanted to buy some pornography, it has been a while and your Mum isn't what she used to be. At work all the lads are raving about this stuff you can pick up on the streets and I thought sure I'll look into it, I even heard rumblings that a couple of your friends were dealing. But to find out my own boy, my smart boy, is just a petty dealer. I thought better of you."

For a moment, Michael felt ten years old again, lambasted for making a mess in his room. Suddenly though he felt it, it overtook him, like it did Tom straight from the beginning. How he had noticed it take over, transform and improve Holly. The pride rose from his feet, he cracked his spine as it travelled there and finally it reached his mind and his mouth.

"Actually father I'm more than a dealer" He looked up, unintentionally menacing. "The dealers work for me; this is MY BUSINESS. You thought more from me? I am earning more money than I know what to do with, I have people doing my bidding, and I have people afraid of me"

For the first time in Michaels twenty-five years, his father looked at him and saw a Man staring back, more than that, a challenger to leader of the pack. They both knew that now was a decisive moment in their relationship, his father contemplated several different scenarios; Telling the police? He was not a grass. Hit him? He could never raise a hand to his son. Tell his mother? How could he explain how he found out? The worst thing in all these scenarios was they all left his son in serious trouble and himself without porn, he decided to go with his gut and his heart.

"I'm proud of you," Michael almost argued back until he processed what he had just heard. "I was gutted someone so smart wasted getting a degree for so long, and now look at you! My boy is respected and successful, it also pleases me that I know you are sensible and will manage to stay out of trouble. Come here." Michaels Dad pulled his son in hard by the shoulders for a manly embrace before pulling him back and gently tapping Michaels face with his palm. Michael finally felt worthy being next in line as man of the family. "But Son" There was always a but when it came to one of Michael's father's speeches "You must tell Tara, trust me from experience. Lie to your woman and they will make you go bald."

"Well that is pot calling the kettle black," Michael mockingly said breaking free from his Dads grip.

"I don't understand?" His father responded quizzing the accusation.

"This whole empire we've created came from your porn you had hidden from Mum and the authorities"

"What porn?" Dad grew even more confused.

"When Tom and I dug up the pond we found your stash of magazines and DVD's! That was our original stock." Michael was beginning to grow concerned by how honest his Dads face was, who replied with an uncertain laugh.

"I have no idea what you are talking about Mikey, your mother made me get rid of my stash long before the ban came into effect, in fact the only way I could get away with it was if I took the laptop into the bathroom and used the internet." Michael looked just a tad disgusted by his father's admission but he was assured his Dad was telling the truth.

"Maybe it was there from before, or some chancer hid it there instead of handing it over or destroying. Either way you're right, I should tell Tara before she finds out."

"Good lad." His Dad took him by the shoulder and they walked the alleyway side by side, as they disappeared into the darkness his asked Michael "Are you handing the porn over or not?"

"Not now Dad."

"What I paid good money for that, also in future I want discount." They bickered like back and forth like this for the rest of their journey home.

Michael never entered the house when they got back. Instead, he stood in the doorway on the phone to Tara, the poor girl was half-asleep and confused at the midnight call but when Michael said he needed to see her right now, that the love he had for her was so much he had to tell her something that could not wait any longer. She obliged and when Michaels father literally chucked the keys to his Silver saloon car for Michael to borrow he was on this way round to his fiancé's.

Tara was waiting by the front door patiently. Her eyes bleary and her natural curls of her hair tried to escape her scalp in every direction. She had her arms nested comfortably up in the sleeves of her furry pink dressing gown and she leaned peacefully against the door, when the headlights of the car came towards her she shielded her eyes and slowly went to meet Michael, climbing into the front seat.

"What is wrong Mikey?" Tara yawned as she leaned her head on Michaels lap and he stroked her hair "You've got me worried. What is so urgent?"

"Ok, please just hear me out and let me finish before interrupting." Michael sighed and Tara obliged, she listened to all of it, to the beginning, by the middle she was no longer half asleep, her eyes were wide open and she stared at her engagement ring wondering what will be the end as she soaked in everything she was being told. How he felt successful after years of regret for not going to university, how he finally had a purpose in this world, newfound respect and admiration, and how this was going to be the foundation for their happy life together. Michael looked down at the head still resting in his lap waiting for Tara to say anything, and after a short while she stirred.

"Michael." She started; it was unusual for her to call him Michael. Her voice was scarce of any emotion or tiredness "I don't know what this silliness is, but if what you are saying is true, then you are breaking the law. I do not know what phase you are going through but I cannot be involved in it. You need to work out what you want."

"I want both." Michael said choking on his words, he tried to stroke Tara's curls again but she flinched her head away.

"You can't have both, I think what's best is that I go back off to university and we spend some time apart and you can decide what you really want, this doesn't have to be the end." She sat up from Michaels lap as he looked through the windscreen shocked and into the distance, he did not really know what to expect from telling Tara, but he was certain he would get away with what he wanted. He did not know what to say and it was not until Tara slammed the car door shut he noticed she had left the car and was scrapping her pink slippers across the ground and back into her house. Michael, defeated started the engine and was about to set off back to his parents when suddenly he was dismayed to see sat in the passenger's seat the golden glimmer of the engagement ring that only a few weeks earlier he had placed on Tara's hand.

CHAPTER 17

Kneecap respected and enjoyed his position within Holly, Michaels and Tom's criminal empire. It did not impede on his photography work; in fact, it gave him a more stable income. He saw himself as an underboss. Not so much to Tom, who figuratively speaking is the boss as he founded the project; Kneecap often assumed Tom would refer to himself as the Don if he had it his way. However, he appreciated the fact Holly and Michael respected and requested his council, and that he can have input into their industry and enjoyed having a higher rank than Simon or Adam.

Morally, he hated breaking the law yet with his own cultural background, his artistic integrity and his experiences at University, he encouraged freedom of expression. Taking the option for people to enjoy erotic entertainment away from the people, professionally made subject matter in particular, was wrong in his eyes. So here, he was fighting the good fight, a fight that was rapidly turning into a war as demands from their once small operation were coming in from all over Kent. At the rapid rate of expansion, Kneecap could forecast soon that they would be serving in Sussex and Essex by autumn and even breach London by the end of the year.

He hoped that by then his school nickname would escape him. When he set up his photography business, he realised how few people, even those who had known him his whole life, knew his real name of Nadeem. It never bothered him up until that point, but when he handed out business cards and people asked if Nadeem was a relative he felt like his career was being squashed and hindered before it got a chance to develop. He contemplated naming his company after his nickname but thought against it because if he wouldn't hire a professional photographer who was named after a part of the human body, then why would anyone else? He may as well set up a graphics design company named after his earlobe whilst he was at it. It further troubled him now with his life in organised crime. He felt a nickname as if Kneecap was a caricature of old fashioned gangsters and that he would never get serious recognition until he shifted it. Nadeem shook his head back to life as he came out of his daydream; these were the thoughts that grew in the flowerbed of his brain when his mind was given time to wander down the garden path. He sat at a bus stop in the centre of Queensmouth town. It was approaching the middle of the day and the town was crowded with people, the church car park behind contained the midweek market with stallholders almost pleading for custom.

"HAREEFURAPOOND" is all you could hear every thirty seconds or so which came loudly from the runt of a stallholder overbearing all other market noise. You could just about decipher that the little old fruit and veg stall owner offering out apples three for a pound and others must have cracked the code as well as a horde of customers were throwing money at him.

Opposite where he sat, and across the road where cars slowly managed to go through the traffic lights two by two to get to the shops for supplies to survive a flood, was the job centre and courthouse where it was commonplace to see the same people flitter between the two. To the right was a bar, which struggled to make its mind up what it was, it looked like a wine bar but the patrons were drinking beer in the middle of day standing outside smoking in their uniformed tracksuits. Between these buildings was the long high street that contained shops all the way, until you could not see anymore and shoppers looked like insects.

There was a reason Kneecap was sat out in public, although he did not want to be seen as a corner dweller he felt it was smarter and safer to meet a new customer in public. He could visually vet the person as they approached, he could disappear into the crowd, and it did not involve shitting on their own doorsteps by bringing them to the Bunker. In all honesty, this was a different approach from the norm so Kneecap wanted a busy day full of people. Procedure was that before they meet a random customer, most were obliged to be introduced and vouched for by a current client; job history and photographs were also required. What made this unique was that this potential customer had approached them directly and discreetly and they had nothing to go on other than the fact he was from one of the neighbouring cities but proved he had a lot of money. When he approached Kneecap via email he chose to ignore it until a second email of a bank statement containing an account holding a figure ending with numerous zeroes arrived in his inbox, so after conversing with Holly and Michael about the potential profit it was agreed Kneecap would arrange to meet the man first. He was apprehensive that he had to do it alone, Adam and Simon were currently on an errand up north and it was mutually decided not to implicate Tom, Michael or Holly, so he knew it was the best decision.

In the nest of insect shoppers, Kneecap could spot the black crow walking down the high street standing high above everyone else seeking out the man he was to meet for the first time and arrange a deal. Kneecap immediately recognised his shiny head and moustachioed swagger but was not entirely prepared for him to be so humungous, and Nadeem only got more intimidated the closer he got until they were almost face to chest.

Kneecap couldn't work out if he was scared or in awe but he was soon put at ease away he was called by his real name.

"Nadeem?" the soothing voice said offering a hand. Kneecap accepted the strong handshake and soon his new acquaintance joined him by sitting by his side "nice to finally meet you."

"Likewise, sorry for the need to do things like this but we can never be too careful." Kneecap said apologetically, looking straight ahead, as the people pacing around town were oblivious to the meeting taking place at the bus stop.

"So you don't mind discussing your business and product out in public" The big, black man replied somewhat confused.

"I haven't said anything, I'm just waiting for a bus with my friend Mr. Foreland" Kneecap replied defensively, yet he gave him the benefit of the doubt. It was his first time and perhaps did not know the delicacy of their dealings.

"So how do we speak about the kind of product you have, how much you have, and how much I can buy, you know I have the money." He continued to goad but still spoke as part friend and part businessman but this set alarm bells off in Nadeem's head. He had seen enough American cop shows where drug dealers were caught out by a wiretap to cause paranoia

"That's why we have this initial meeting sir" Nadeem kept his manners, there was still a slim chance of a major deal here "I meet you, get first impressions, then go off to my bosses, we discuss the situation, then arrange another meet. Plus whoever initially put you in contact must have given you a shrewd idea."

"True." Foreland nodded impressed, and this was when he realised what the man in the hospital bed said was true, this was no amateur operation. "I have a shrewd idea, and now I hope since we have had this meeting, you can go back to your bosses Adam and Simon and discuss me."

"Adam and Simon are not my bosses" Nadeem said part annoyed at the accusation.

"Oh are they not?" Foreland said before doubling his height advantage over Nadeem by standing with a half grin, satisfied he had started the game of cat and mouse he loved so much. Kneecap sat in a trance as he watched the large man strut off back into the distance, prematurely ending their meeting.

"Damn he was cool, wonder if he is gay, Adam would love him." Kneecap thought to himself as he noticed the large frame of Foreland was still visible up until he reached the very top of the high street, once he disappeared from sight Kneecap tried to process everything that just took place and slightly began to panic. "I need to warn the others." and Kneecap stood impatiently waiting for the bus that would take him to headquarters.

CHAPTER 18

Michael did not fancy sitting upstairs with the other dwellers in the bunkers bar and had taken himself and a bottle of scotch into the cellar, he rolled up his shirt sleeves before slumping into one of the chairs surrounding the desk and swigging from the bottle. He had forgotten he did not like scotch and he coughed from the burn. Expelling his tongue from his mouth from disgust and his eyes watered, he looked around the rest of the cellar for another kind of beverage before returning to his seat with only a bottle of cola. He made a combination of the two drinks, his face showed he still was not keen but at least this time as he sipped it did not dissolve a hole in his gullet.

It was midweek so upstairs the pub was by no means heaving, but there were enough patrons for a lively atmosphere and for Holly to have Chloe work the shift with her. It was also nice to be able to breath between drink demands. There was a visiting pool team playing the Bunker's home team in a league match so noise level was always at a high as banter was exchanged but nothing was too heavy or vicious and the jukeboxes music could still be heard in the background even though it was at a moderate volume. Chloe was all smiles as she got a round of applause, cheers and whistles as she bought out plates of rolls, chips and sausages. She was doing her sexy bum wiggle walk while her pink flowery jump suit clung to her. Yet Holly was not convinced all the cheers were for Chloe considering the stomachs on some of the pool players, one of the visiting team members did ask Chloe crudely however if she liked munching sausage.

Holly herself was slowly getting used to the constant compliments and flirtatious comments. Her new confidence and style was noticeable and the purple dress she wore with her hair straightened were causing eyes to switch between the two girls. This caused a major customer debate over which they preferred out of the two barmaids, it was the toughest decision a lot of them made since deciding on beer or spirits for their first drink. Holly then noticed Michael was no longer hunched on the bar stool in his depressed state and she rightly assumed he had ventured off downstairs. It had been well over a week since Michael split from Tara, and Tom and Holly had tried endlessly to help cheer him up.

Tom was playing darts with one of his old school mates, Holly decided to interrupt his little game and try to persuade him to head down with her to the basement. She forgot to add to her request that it was to cheer their moping friend up.

"Is that an invitation?" Holly loved the fact Tom was now his old self around her again, he was back to flirting with her in his own way and Holly now knew how much she had missed it. She frantically took one of the darts out of his hand and jumped back with a big cheeky smile.

"I'll throw it at you if you don't come now." Holly said playfully pretending to chuck it.

"What if it was like Cupid's arrow and made me fall in love with you?" Tom damned himself for again letting his real feelings slip through his normal crude flirts. Holly's playful demeanour stopped as the arm holding the dart drooped to her side and they both avoided eye contact for a split second as Holly realised more and more how much she felt the same. This time Tom decided to take the lead and end the awkward moment with a witty retort by punching his mate in the arm and saying "Ha, it will take more than a dart for that, more like a fucking spear."

His friend laughed dumbly not even noticing the tense moment Tom and Holly just had, Holly looked at Tom with her eyes big and thankful and Tom put his arm around her in a manner a mate would and led the way away from the dart board.

"Come on Holly let's go see Happy." Tom was oblivious to Holly looking up at him the whole time as he fraternised with other patrons on their way round the back of the bar.

They go unnoticed by Michael as the two enter the cellar. Michael was preoccupied still sat at the desk with a half empty whiskey and coke sitting idly in front of him on the desk at arm's length. Michael's hands clenched each side of the seat he sat in as he thrashed his head attempting to sing.

"HERE I GO AGAIN ON MY OWN." echoed viciously around the cellar. Holly struggled to contain laughter but just about managed to suppress it, Tom automatically grabbed his air guitar and went to town playing make believe chords, his hands looking like a tyrannosaurus having a seizure. He opened his mouth wanting to join his friend in the ballad but Holly grabbed his wrist looked at Tom with a finger over her lips indicating him to keep quiet.

Holly was the first to approach, walking behind Michael and startling him as she calmly said his name, his head turned and he raised his glass with a loud cheering noise greeting his friends.

"Michael, how much have you drunk?" she asked concerned, Michael picked up the bottle of scotch from between his legs and Tom laughed.

"Fucking lightweight," his friend jested. "Scotch?" thankfully it was said with enough friendliness that Michael lifted his hands up to say oh well. His two colleagues joined him at the table grabbing seats; Tom sat on his seat back to front. Michael confessed that he had been missing Tara.

"Just pretend you are still together but she is permanently at university." Tom interjected with useless advice that earned him a punch in the arm from Holly but a drunken grin from Michael.

Nevertheless, what played on his mind the most was that he felt guilty. Guilty that he effectively chose their business and the money over her and he was worried that that was the person he had become, full of greed.

"Don't be ridiculous." Holly snapped, "You are not selfish or shallow, everything you do is for us and your friends. Who was the one who met your Dad so no one else was implicated? You! Maybe sub consciously; you wanted to end it with Tara, you had been together a long time but how often were you together? Even when she had chances to come back from uni she would delay it. Maybe you know you deserve someone more devoted."

"Like Adam." Tom pointlessly added again, unable to help himself with a taunt, Holly told him to shut up. Meanwhile Michael seemed lost in concentration dissecting Holly's words, he slowly nodded seemingly in agreement but did not tell the other two what he was really feeling.

The all too familiar scene of Kneecap bumbling through the cellar door and landing on his arse interrupted Michael's moment of clarity. The trio looked at each other raising their eyebrows, tutting and shaking their heads astonished at how many times, the same person can forget the steps that lead to the cellar door as Kneecap climbed back to his feet.

"What the hell do you want now Kneecap?" Tom delightfully welcomed him in a way only he could without causing offence. Kneecap rubbed his eyes with his hairy hands and pulled down his cheeks showing fear in his face. The other three's minor annoyance soon subsided and they look worried and concerned. This would only escalate as a stuttering Kneecap revealed all about the rendezvous with the potential client he had just a couple of hours prior. He explained his suspicions about the man and how he was acting, how he managed to be intimidating even with his calm approach, he revealed how much this threat knew about the operation and that they should not trust him or his money.

Tom looked confused and angry, Holly seemed to be calculating mentally and Michael was suddenly sober. Tensions were high down in the Bunker's basement and matters were not helped when the handle on the door opened. Adam and Simon were away and the only other people with access to the cellar were presently in the room. The creak of the door literally made Kneecap jump inches off the ground, Holly stood behind Tom who armed himself with Michael's whiskey bottle. He held a protective arm across Holly's legs and Michael rubbed his eyes and stumbled as he stood. As the door flung open five screams deafened ten ears as Chloe entered the room,

she was as horrified as the rest of them as Tom nearly lunged at her.
Michael nearly fainted into Kneecaps arms who propped him against the
wall.

"You scared the life out of us girl" Holly said breathing heavily, Chloe
just gave her a look suggesting that she hardly appreciated the greeting she
received either.

"Oh really?" Chloe snapped back. Holly then asked what Chloe was
doing down here and she obliged "There is a bloke up here that looks
funny, a big black guy"

"And you think he looked funny?" Holly quizzed the racial undertones.

"That's not what I mean." Chloe said holding her chest shocked she
would be accused of such a thing "I have a thing for black men" she added
rather unnecessarily "It's what he is asking, he is asking a lot of questions,
about whether a Nadeem is here? Or if Adam and Simon are about, and he
is asking about whether I know of any unlawful dealings in the pub."

"And what did you say?" Tom said holding his arms out impatient.

"Well I said other than the porn being sold here, nothing."

"What?" Michael screamed, climbing to his feet almost now completely
sober through shock. "You know?"

"I'm not stupid Michael." Her hands rested on her waist. Chloe was
growing tired of accusations.

"Chloe this isn't the time for jokes, what did you really say?" Tom was
calm yet stern and Chloe could tell if Tom was not in the mood for joking
then the situation was serious, she nodded and spoke with her head down.

"I told him Adam and Simon haven't been here in a while and that I had
never even heard of a Nadeem"

"I'm Nadeem." Kneecap hissed, but was ignored by the others who had
no time for petty conversations, Chloe however responded confused.

"What's that? Indian for Kneecap?" Tom was the only one who
acknowledged her reply unable to contain his laugh so he spat it out.

"Right what exactly does he know?" Holly interjected talking directly to
Kneecap.

"He knows that me, Adam and Simon are involved with distributing porn
somehow, and obviously has an inkling we operate from here, or he at least
knows we drink here. I'm certain he has no idea you three are involved."

After a short moment of deliberation, it was decided that Holly as
manager of the pub should go up and find out whom this person was asking
questions and find out as much as she could. Tom decided she should undo
the top button on purple dress by just undoing it for her, the others wished
her luck as they were to hide out of the way. Holly adjusted the bottom of
her dress straightening it and headed up to the bar, only Chloe joined her.

Holly went straight for the kill heading immediately for the log like arms resting open palmed on the bar. His head caught her eye instantly and he looked down over the top of his glasses at her. He stroked his goatee with his right hand the way he always did when either a woman caught his eye or a clue presented itself in a case, the purple dress she was wearing showed curves that all Detective Foreland could do was appreciate. Before he could even decide that he preferred this woman to the one he previously had spoken to at the bar he was hit with the verbal jousts.

"My colleague here says, you are harassing her with questions? She also says you have not ordered a drink. So if you want to speak to someone speak to me. I am in charge here." The aggression and fire caught Foreland and even Chloe off guard; he is normally the dominant one in conversations and now this powerful, young, beautiful woman was the one attacking him. As he watched her grow impatient, he guessed she was a voice of reason so he introduced himself, was honest with her, and explained his theory that her establishment was being used as a hub for people distributing illegal erotic material.

"So? Are you not meant to go through proper procedure? Instead, you choose to come to my pub and snoop around with no warrant and harass my staff and myself. So I ask you one more time Detective Foreland. Are you having a drink?"

It was at that point the detective's giant chest grew tight; he felt something suddenly grab at his heart and he realised it was the woman that stood before him. In that split instant he decided to choose relations over his professionalism, but for once it was not lust. He wanted to get to know this woman, the first he had ever encountered that he thought strong enough to match him on his level. He had been with far too many women over the years, many involved with cases he had worked on, but this was the first time any of them made think thoughts of leaving his wife.

"Apologies" Holly's attack had no effect on his voice "I did not mean to intrude or be rude, I went on a hunch and I wholeheartedly say sorry." He buttoned up his jacket and went to take his leave, yet he turned slapping the bar and approached it again. "I would like to leave you my personal number; I would like to get to know you Miss?"

"Just call me Holly" she said abruptly "And I…" A giant finger placed on her lips, which took her off guard and interrupted her. The Detective decided to at least make the first move regardless of its success, and did not give a chance of rejection.

"Either way I will leave my number here." He took a pen from his jacket pocket and his card. He crossed off his work number, instead wrote his personal mobile number, slid it across the bar before giving a strong wave, and slowly and smoothly walked towards the pubs exit, customers in the pub felt obliged to move out of his way as he gracefully walked past them. Before leaving he turned only his head like an owl to soak in one last look at Holly, which did not go unnoticed, he smiled a half smile before leaving the pub entirely. Holly and Chloe looked at each other with their mouths open wide with shock.

"You going to text him?" Chloe said fast and excitedly.

"Chloe, remember who he is?"

"Oh yeah" Chloe slapped the air with a giggle "So what do we do now."

"I think we need to tell the guys downstairs what just happened and come up with a plan." Holly sucked her bottom lip curiously thinking about everything that had just happened before picking up Detective Forelands phone number and putting it down the top of her dress.

CHAPTER 19

"Yellow car." Twack! Adam's fist went flying into Simon's skinny arm. It was already showing bruising. Worst of all he was holding onto the steering wheel and his little red car swerved a little on impact. A tad bit dangerous on the motorway.

"Stop doing that." Simon protested frowning, his forehead wrinkled in annoyance.

"It's the rules of the road." Adam said turning to face his friend who was concentrating on the busy conveyor belt of fast cars ahead of him.

"But we have been on the road for four hours, we've literally seen thousands of cars, if you hit me every time you see a yellow car I'm going to need my arm chopping off." Simon was shaking at the wheel of the car while Adam looked out of his passenger side window like an abandoned puppy watching the cars zoom by as his legs were propped up on the dashboard. All they had seen for the past few hours was vehicles coming and going and the long seemingly never-ending road. Motorways were boring and at Simon's insistence, they did not stop at a service station, not even for a little Chef. He promised Adam that once they were in Leeds they could have a beer, a burger and chill out for a bit. Simon reminded Adam that they both agreed to get this trip done all in one day.

They were going into this business trip with some apprehension; they were off to liaise with someone known only as 'Big Daddy'. If rumours were true, this contact had the biggest collection of digital porn in England. An endless supply, which catered to all sorts of genres and fetishes. He had been boasting about it over the internet and took joy in not sharing any of his wealth. This had proved to be his downfall, disgruntled internet users informed the authorities of his activities and they were hot on his tail. When this 'Big Daddy' discovered the distribution operation going on in the southeast, he saw an opportunity to get out of this sticky situation and make money at the same time.

He managed, through contacts online, to track down and reach out to Kneecap who listened and presented 'Big Daddy's' proposal to Holly, Michael and Tom. He would hand over everything he owned. In return he wanted a small percentage of monthly profit that the gang thought was laughably small they decided to snatch his hand off. Adam and Simon were sent up north to Leeds to check out if this was true. Simon was wary at first but Michael explained to him in detail what the plan was and he felt at ease. Adam was sold the moment Tom said that they wanted to send their top soldiers up there to complete the deal.

"Why are we still driving? We passed the sign for Sheffield ages ago." Adam moaned rasping his lips with a sigh.

"It's at least sixty miles from Sheffield to Leeds. Do you have to moan the whole journey?" Simon was beginning to get annoyed with Adams persistent moaning. "If it's not the distance you're complaining about being hungry, if it's not hunger you need a slash and so on. It won't be too much longer I promise"

"I just assumed once we got to Yorkshire we would be there, I got excited when we saw the sign for Sheffield, but nope still we stay on this poxy motorway."

"That's nonsense though isn't it, take Kent for example, the two biggest cities, Canterbury and Maidstone aren't exactly next door to each other." Simon stared over at Adam whenever he could to show his contempt.

"I suppose when you put it like that" Adam defeated turned his face to once again stare out of the window at the nothingness. A kind of cabin fever was taking over the two friends locked in a car all this time and they were driving one another insane, whatever one did it managed to annoy the other. Simon sensing this indicated and pulled into the outside lane and put his foot down in an attempt to get to Leeds as quick as possible. He was relieved when he heard the deep wheezing breaths oozing from Adams mouth as he snored after falling asleep. Simon smiled knowing he finally had peace and said to himself.

"I never thought the sound of snoring would sound so beautiful."

At long last they made it to Leeds and Simon had to physically wake Adam by shaking him in his sleep much to his friend's annoyance. Adam tried to swat Simon away but once he was awake and Simon explained the need to direct him he grunted and wiped the drool from his mouth and reached for his phone loading up the map application.

"Thank god for that" Simons said, "this city driving lark is confusing. I spent five minutes driving in a fucking bus lane without realising and I've been around the same roundabout so many times I'm surprised we don't suffer from vertigo."

Fortunately, with Adams assistance they found the Leeds city centre coach station where they were told to park up and wait for further instructions. Life up north did not seem too different to what they were used to down south except for greyer skies and a language where plurals did not seem to exist. They both stepped out of Simon's car and stretched. They made it seem like their few hour journey was an expedition or a grand voyage, both clad in tracksuits, with messy hair and six o'clock shadows. Simon texted the contact number letting them know they arrived then he paused for thought, Adam instinctively knew what he was thinking and also paused as it dawned on both of them that they really had no idea who or what they were planning to meet.

"So, uh, what do you think this Big Daddy is going to be like?" asked Adam as Simon finished sending his text message.

"I honestly have no clue, I'm glad there are two of us though. What about you?"

"To be honest I'm picturing a black guy with a perm, lots of jewellery, a green shiny suit with tiger printed trim and a feathered hat." Adam replied his hand scratching the fluff on his chin in concentration.

"So you think this guy, in the middle of Yorkshire, will turn out to essentially be a stereotypical 1970's pimp from Harlem?"

"Well why would he call himself Big Daddy?"

"Any reason, remember the wrestler in the eighties? He was hardly an African American pimp, and maybe, just maybe he is a Big Daddy?" Simon stretched out tall to indicate a tall person then cradled an imaginary baby in his arms to signify the daddy aspect.

"Then why isn't he called Giant Father?" Adam was more curious than argumentative but their discussion about whom they would be meeting was interrupted by a text from the person in question. Simon read the text message and relayed the instructions to his partner.

"He wants us to meet in a McDonalds inside a shopping centre, he says he has a picture of us so knows who to meet and he will join us at whatever table we are sat at. Do you still have that map app up? We can use that."

"Of course, but the first pub we see afterwards we're going for a drink." Simon nodded in agreement and they set off. It was a little more than a fifteen-minute walk to the shopping centre and they noted how much busier and multi-cultural it was up here compared to their small coastal town. Once they arrived at the shopping centre, the fast food restaurant was easily found and they entered. Adam instinctively went and ordered chicken nuggets while Simon got straight to business and found a table for them to sit at. Adam joined him with his food and drink and handed a cheeseburger to Simon, which he opened up and bit into appreciating the gift.

Simon paused mid bite of his burger thanks to the elbow nudging of Adam beside him, burger almost fell from his lips as the two of them were gawking at one of the lined up customer's glinting emerald suit. It belonged to a skinny black man with an even darker curly haircut. He held a cane, which did not serve a purpose other than aiding his strut and he ordered his food in a New York accent.

"What did I tell you?" Adam whispered proud in victory as they both continued to stare at the man awaiting his food. Other than the lack of tiger print, a feathered hat and the jewellery, what stood before them was identical to Adam's description of what Big Daddy would look like. Even Simon was beginning to think he was wrong to doubt his friend.

They jumped out of their skins as their view was obstructed by the close up sight of a hairy stomach escaping from beneath a grey t-shirt. It spoke their names and as both men slowly veered their sight up towards the face that owned the belly, the reason they were asked to meet in a McDonalds became clear.

In front of them was a fair haired, balding, obese man in his late thirties. His chin wobbled as his squeaky voice spoke and you could hear and see his heart struggling to pump blood around his body. He wheezed as he managed to squeeze himself between a chair and the table where he placed his three meals; including a milkshake, two burgers, a large fries and a chicken wrap.

"Jesus, now the name makes sense." Adam whispered from the corner of his mouth with Simon agreeing discretely as they watched their contact clean thick brown framed glasses that when he put them back on it made his eyes bulge out of his head.

The three exchanged greetings and quietly discussed what they knew of each other. Big Daddy, who still did not divulge his real name, gave a brief rundown of his history and how he came about obtaining this much pornography. He explained that Big Daddy was his internet handle, and openly admitted he was a bully when it came to the World Wide Web. When Simon said he was just an online troll Big Daddy seemed to take offence. The out of shape man told them how in real life he had no purpose, no reputation, how people did not even know he existed. So instead, he gave his life and health over to becoming an internet tough guy where people actually feared him. Adam and Simon nearly threw up their meals when Big Daddy explained that porn was the only intimacy he had ever had in his life and the closest he will ever get to seeing a woman naked. When rumblings of the ban on erotic entertainment started to become serious, he used his online reputation to acquire as much pornography as possible. His squeaky voice grew more sinister and his eyes became more evil as he visibly enjoyed talking about how he blackmailed and forced internet users into hacking into British, German, American, Dutch and Brazilian porn sites then ordering them to send them to be downloaded onto one of three sixteen terabyte hard drives situated in Big Daddy's bedroom.

"So in total I have in my possession forty-eight terabyte's of pornography, all genres, and all orientations, anything to cater to anybody's needs. Looking back, I think I got power hungry." He chortled.

He led the two soldiers, who were trying to comprehend just how many hours of porn this man had, to his silver estate car parked down an alley.

He popped the trunk of the car and the short journey had Big Daddy puffing from being out of breath. In the back was a red plastic container, he peeled back the lid to reveal three hard drives no bigger than mobile phones.

"Here gents is the reason your friends are going to pay me a percentage a month."

"Is that it?" Adam quizzed "All that porn is stored on them three things?" He pointed accusingly in the trunk. Simon picked one up, confirmed the sizes of the hard drives, and put Adam at ease letting him know that all that content would fit on the hard drives.

It was time for the business meeting to conclude, Adam lifted the container from the car and Simon shook Big Daddy's hand goodbye as he squeezed into the driver's seat. Simon cringed at the sweat left on his hand from the shake. They made their way back to the car park and loaded the merchandise into Simon's car who knew he had a promise to keep.

"Right" he said to Adam. "I promised you a beer."

"To be honest I just want to head back now and see what's on them hard drives."

"Come on, I saw a couple of blokes enjoying a pint around the corner. We're only having one, besides I think you will like this place." It did not take much to persuade Adam and his eyes lit up like the Blackpool lights when he read the sign on the side of the pub. 'The Cock Pit: Leeds biggest gay bar'.

CHAPTER 20

Only two colours seemed to exist in Holly's bedroom, Purple and White. The curtains were a dark aubergine colour and were drawn; the bed frame was white leather with a neatly folded lilac quilt lying comfortably on top of it. Flowery canvasses hung from the purple painted walls with a snow like rug covering the grey carpet. Beside her bed was a wooden chest of drawers on the right and wardrobe/vanity unit combination to the left. Everything was neat and tidy.

Michael quietly entered the room looking around for the chest of drawers and started to head towards it, as per Holly's instructions. In his right hand was Holly's mobile phone, it vibrated twice signalling a text message, Michael already knew who it was from. He stopped half way across the room and looked back at the open white door where Tom stood as if a barrier prevented him from entering.

"Come on Tom" Michael said directing with his head. "I thought this would be your Mecca."

"I don't play bingo." Tom said like a moody child with his arms folded across his chest.

"I meant a kind of religious pilgrimage… never mind" Michael read the text message on Holly's phone and carried on "It's from the detective."

"I don't like this one bit" Tom said entering Holly's bedroom, a dream becoming a nightmare. He pulled Michael's arm in front of his face so he could read the text "I did not think this is how I would first get to see Hol's room."

"Come on" there was a comforting tone in Michaels voice "You know we have to do this. For all our sakes."

Michael had picked himself up lately, this drama with the detective had given him something to focus on other than Tara and protecting his business and friends was top priority, it was a complete character swap for Tom to be the reluctant party for once. Only Michael, Tom and Holly knew of the plan to rid themselves of the detective. They did not want to get anyone else involved, especially as he was already sniffing around the pub and Kneecap.

Michael opened the top drawer, again following Holly's instructions. It was her underwear drawer and Michael tried not to rummage too much and pulled out a black laced bra with a pair of black laced underwear with a white floral print on the front and not much around the back. Tom tried to pretend he was above looking but still peeked with intrigue from the corner of his eye. Delicately Michael placed them on the lilac quilt and smoothed them out.

"I still don't get why we have to use her own underwear" Tom objectified still staring at the bed "place two dust masks close together and bang! You have a convincing bra; I have two in the van."

"Tom, we're trying to be seductive. If we want the result we need we have to be convincing, we want this detective to think Holly wants him." Michael used Hollys phone to take a picture of the underwear and sent it to Foreland along with the caption 'Should I wear this tonight, or would you prefer them off xxx'. Not long after the message was sent, Holly came springing up the stairs and entered her bedroom fresh out of the bath. Her wet hair clung to her neck and back and a light pink towel covered her from her knees to the top of her chest, she still had droplets of water on her that made her shine in the light, to Tom she looked like an angel yet he could not look at her for long. Holly's phone vibrated in Michael's hand again and he read the incoming message.

"I asked the detective if he preferred you in or out of your underwear and he has just replied with 'Maybe we can try both, see you at 8 xxx' so I think he is keen."

"Well if he is lucky he might get both" Holly laughed; she was only joking but soon regretted it when she saw Tom's thunderous face. "well that doesn't give me long to get ready, you two don't want to be here when he turns up, so leave and let me get ready." They did not need telling twice and they let themselves out of Holly's house, Tom did not even say bye, he couldn't.

Alone in her house she had to kill time. Holly was too restless and fidgety to watch anything on the television so instead she put some music on at a low volume and wandered aimlessly around the lower floor of her house, she popped into the kitchen and poured herself a glass of white wine. She very seldom drank wine but she felt it was appropriate with the classy dress she was wearing. She lined herself with a black, pencil dress that hugged smoothly to her arms, chest, hips and legs, she was worried it might be too tight and show off her curves too much but as she studied herself in the mirror she felt comfortable and confident that is suited her. The dress had a curved neckline that started on her right shoulder and ended just above her heart, leaving a bit of skin visible on the left side of her chest. Sipping her wine, she became anxious as the butterflies emerged from the cocoons in her stomach. She sat on her cream leather sofa, closed her eyes and took deep breaths, while the wine glass was held firmly in her hand.

This managed to calm her and before she knew it, her waiting time had elapsed and with a thump on the door, Holly knew it was time to put their plan to work. She took a lesson from the blokes down the pub and downed the rest of her wine in one and disgraced herself by letting out a very un-lady like belch, she was just relieved it was before she opened the door. Once it was open, standing in her doorway was the Detective, naturally tall and proud like a stallion he had on a pale blue turtleneck jumper with a navy blue suit over the top. Holly gulped when she saw the bouquet of roses sprouting from his giant hand; she took them and leaned up to kiss him on the cheek, even in her white heels she had to tip toe to barely reach his face.

"I've never been bought flowers on a date before." Holly said with a smile, and it was true. In all her years and the many disastrous dates, she had been on, not once had anyone thought to buy her flowers, in fact neither had they just said wear a fancy dress and be ready for eight. Both of which Foreland had done, the only person to wine and dine her was her enemy, yet he did not know she was, yet.

The date itself was of little note, small idle chitchat filled the breaks between eating. They were in a small yet classy Italian restaurant that overlooked the Queensmouth harbour, Holly didn't even know this place existed and when she asked Foreland how an out of towner knew about it. He looked her coldly into her eyes waving a spaghetti wrapped fork and said.

"I'd be a pretty lousy detective if I couldn't find a decent place to eat; It's my job to find things out… about everything" They looked at each other for a few seconds, Holly felt uncomfortable before the detective laughed and scooped some more food from his plate. "Nah, I saw a leaflet at the hotel I'm staying at." Holly joined in the laughter not wanting to give away how nervous she was.

She soon discovered what Forelands favourite subject to talk about was; himself. Admittedly some of his anecdotes about former cases were interesting; especially the murders and she paid extra attention to recent cases involving the erotic entertainment act, making mental notes on how not to slip up. Overall, she was not bored and time went by steadily until it was time for him to take her home, this moment was the one that she was looking forward to the least.

As expected, the detective offered to walk Holly to her front door and offered her his branch like arms to hang onto, which she accepted.

"I could swing from these like a monkey," Holly said nervously, before adding an impression, when it did not garner a laugh she felt silly. Once the short distance from the car to her front door was made there was the longest silence as the detective was almost seductively trying to hypnotize Holly with his brown eyes staring intently into hers, his right hand started brushing her right arm where Goosebumps started forming. He leaned the long way down so Holly didn't have to tip toe and delicately placed his lips on hers before craning himself back upright, going straight back into his stare. Holly looked away but his left hand gently made her look into his eye once more. That was when she went into action, placing her index finger on his lips.

"Not so fast mister" She said playfully and giggling, "You have to earn more, you have to tempt me." She kissed him on the cheek and pulled her house key out of her small purse.

"I can respect that, I've never liked anything too easy, I prefer a challenge."

"If you can tempt me enough, you'll complete your challenge in no time." and likewise in no time Holly slipped behind the door closed it and dropped to her butt sitting resting against the front door. She waited for his slow heavy footsteps to fade into the distance and heard his car start up and pull away.

"Eugh, what a sleaze." she spouted wiping her mouth on her arm and shuddering, she was thankful for not having to put up with the pretence anymore. Once she regained composure and was back on her feet, she rang Michael to let him know she was back and that all being well everything will go according to plan. Michael confidently said it will and told her he would be on his way after picking Tom up at the pub.

By the time Michael and Tom knocked on her door Holly had received three messages from Detective Foreland, none of which she had opened wanting to wait for her friends. She had also wrapped herself all snug in her pink fluffy robe and was wearing grey boot like slippers, Holly felt so much more comfortable dressed like this then she did in a sexy dress.

Holly was surprised when she answered the door to find Michael alone, if Holly was all wrapped up for the artic Michael was the opposite in blue shorts, trainers and a white t-shirt looking like he just threw on the first things he could find.

"Where is Tom?" Holly asked curiously.

"Well when I got to the pub he had his head down on the bar, completely shitfaced."

"What?" Holly felt flat. "He knew this was important."

"Yeah, I don't think he approved of the plan, when I went to get him he accused me of whoring you out and that I should've just let him kill the detective."

"Oh God"

"And that is just what I could understand; he was speaking a lot of gibberish." Michael was smiling, almost laughing, "He was in one of his classic states."

"I'm not sure this is funny Michael."

"That's why I left him there, as I left he shouted at me 'an angel doesn't need no pimp' but don't worry as I left Chloe was consoling him rubbing his back and she said she would make sure he got home ok."

"That's some small relief, I would rather he was here" Holly looked sad, she wanted Tom with her so that everything was going to work out, she had recently discovered how reassuring she found him. "You know we're all in this together, it's just selfish to go get drunk whilst we do the work"

"Give it up Holly" Michael rolled his eyes "Don't you think after all this is done it's about time you and Tom admitted your feelings for each other to each other, it's as obvious as a bag of nuts warning us it contains traces of nuts."

"Is it that obvious?" Holly said softly playing with her hair.

"To me it is" Michael gave her a paternal like hug "He has been mad about you since school, and you've obviously grown to like him more than just tolerate him."

Holly enjoyed the encouraging cuddle and was smiling into Michael's chest. Now that was out of the way Michael sat down on the leather sofa and said.

"So what's the situation?"

"Well speak of the devil" Holly's phone once again vibrated in her dressing gown pocket and sat down next to Michael with her legs tucked up behind her bottom. "That's four messages he has left now."

"Well" Michael smiled "Let's start at the beginning." They huddled up close on the sofa so they could both see the screen of Holly's mobile phone. Holly looked at Michael with her thumb poised over the open message button, Michael nodded approval, the first message read:

'Thanks for a great evening babe; I look forward to seeing you again xxx'

"He cringes me out so much" Holly said with a shiver "Are you sure he has a wife and kids?"

"That's what we found out" Michael replied, "Married twenty odd years." Holly looked disgusted and scrolled down to the next message:

'Driving home and all I can think about is that it's a shame I never got see that underwear you showed me earlier, I'll have to tempt you sooner rather than later xxx'

"Now he is using his phone whilst driving" Holly vented waving her free arm around "is there any redeeming quality about him?" she said sarcastically prompting a chuckle from Michael. The next message on the list did not have a preview; it was a multimedia message, either a video or a picture. It took a few moments for the message to open. What waited for them in the picture left Michael and Holly gasping and wide eyed. A Half naked Foreland, stood in his bathroom wearing only his turtleneck but what drew the gasps was what the detective was holding in his left hand; his own personal truncheon which was proud and ready to spring into action.

"There's your fucking redeeming quality, Jesus!" Michael exclaimed loudly, he only broke away from the picture to look at his own crotch, making himself feel inferior. "That's got to be bigger than black beauty's."

"Well, that's certainly more than we expected" Holly gulped trying not to become fixated on the giant penis presently on her screen. "We have an explicit picture, his face is in it, and its time stamped. We've got him" Holly had a beaming smile on her face when she turned with excitement to look at Michael who said.

"I never thought I'd be so happy to see a giant cock." Holly laughed but Michael sounded genuinely happy. "If Tom was here you know he would make a remark about Adam wanting to see this." The two of them were so overjoyed that their plan came to fruition that they almost forgot there was another message to check.

Holly's neighbours could be forgiven for thinking that herself and Michael were being slaughtered by a murderer their screams were that loud. Holly slid the phone across the ground away from the two of them and they both raised their legs up on the sofa trying to create as much distance between them and the device. It was like two old women being scared by a mouse. Even though they had just seen Detective Foreland in all his glory they were not prepared for what was included in the last message; a video of the same Half naked Foreland, sprawled on his bed pleasuring himself which could only be described as looking like he was wrestling a baby alligator.

After the initial shock, they both saw the funny side.

"We have him hook, line and sinker," Michael gloriously shouted clenching his fist in celebration then high fiving Holly; pointing at the phone, he carried on "We need copies of the picture and video straight away, digital copies, physical copies, lots! But right now, you need to message him back, telling him you can't wait to see him."

"How soon?" Holly asked as she walked over to collect the phone and started typing away.

"Why waste any time, tomorrow morning sounds good. Tell him to meet you at the pub first thing in the morning, and tell him it will be empty. I will make sure me AND Tom, hangover or not, are there to confront him with you."

"Are you positive confronting him will work? I mean he could still arrest all of us after." Holly sensibly asked.

"I'm positive" Michael was the most confident he had ever been since embarking on this path "From what we know about the man, we are hitting him where it hurts. His ego, he will not want anyone seeing these pictures, it will ruin his career, family and more importantly to him his reputation."

Holly smiled now convinced that this mission of theirs will be a success, she finished typing up her reply and after she sent it handed her phone to Michael in preparation for copying the crude picture and video of Detective Foreland.

CHAPTER 21

Tom could not exactly remember how this girl got into his bed, but he knew for sure that once she was it was a lot of fun for both people, and the start of moving on from Holly and finding someone else to care for. Then the phone rang, any noise at that moment caused Tom's head to feel like a street worker was using a pneumatic drill on it. Bleary eyed he glanced over at the bulge lying next to him and she seemed dead to the world and therefore unfazed by the phone call. The ringing stopped and to Tom the silence felt like he had been induced with morphine and he comfortably slipped his head back on the pillow with a smile. Then the drilling started again, he begrudgingly reached for his phone which took maximum effort, closing one eye he could finally read that it was Michael ringing him, knowing the calls would continue he reluctantly answered the phone, his throat felt so dry and scratchy he felt like the kebab he got on the way home was made from sandpaper. He tried to say hello but instead answered the phone with a growl; in fact, he never managed one word of English the whole conversation. After hanging up, he threw his phone to the end of the bed and leaned on his side ready to go back to sleep.

Suddenly his eyes opened as the contents of the phone call finally sunk in, he sat up too soon which proved to be a big mistake as when he stood up he stumbled backwards onto the bed. He held his hands out to steady himself and shushed himself as he again stared at the lump under the duvet, its only movement being the girl's slow, sleepy, snores.

Using his bedroom wall, bedside unit and whatever else was available to steady himself against he left the room. Wearing just a pair of pale yellow boxer shorts, he shortly returned with two glasses of water, he plopped one down on the floor by the side where the girl was sleeping; he sat just in front of her holding his glass of water. Gulping it down he shook the bulge, gently at first, but when that did not get a response he shook more erratically.

Finally, a head emerged from the duvet, its brown and blonde highlighted hair curled naturally. Propping herself up on her hands she turned her head, took one look at Tom's bed hair, which looked like it had had a fight with itself, and his bloodshot eyes and she rolled onto her back giggling.

"What's so funny Chloe?" Tom said playfully to the barmaid that looked after, consoled and bought him home last night. He pulled the duvet back revealing her to be wearing his Queensmouth F.C football top as a nightgown; she pulled it down over her knees.

"Don't peek Thomas." Chloe offered with a wink.

"Don't stretch my shirt!" He replied pouncing on top of Chloe tickling her as she wagged her legs frantically, both were giggling hysterically, the laughter momentarily curing Tom's hangover when suddenly Tom remembered something and stopped. He stared into Chloe's hazel eyes, planted a kiss on her forehead, and stroked her curls behind her ears.

"Thank you for last night" He said sentimentally.

"That's ok Thomas" She replied enjoying the closeness of their bodies.

"Nobody ever calls me Thomas, not even my parents."

"Oh Sorry." Chloe was worried she said something wrong but Tom cut her apology off quickly.

"No I like it." Smiling he went for another kiss this time softly on her lips, before swinging his legs around to the floor, standing up and starting to look for some clothes. "Look Chlo, Michaels going to be here in a minute, so we have to get ready" Tom slipped on a pair of light blue jeans, the first thing he could find as well as a creased green, blue, white and red t-shirt. He watched Chloe put on her black leggings in the mirror as he attempted to control his hair and put it back into the flick he had grown accustomed to. She turned catching Tom's reflection and putting the collar up on his football shirt she said.

"Can I keep this shirt? It's so nice to wear to bed." Tom shuffled over to Chloe and put his hand on her waist tugging at the shirt gently.

"You can't take it" He said sternly "But, you could always stay over again perhaps and wear it." Chloe beamed at the suggestion and accepted the compromise.

"Well how about tonight?" She asked and Tom agreed saying it was a good idea.

About half an hour later, Michael and Tom arrived at the pub. On the journey from Tom's he got Michael to drop a now dressed Chloe home, Michael did not pry into why she was at Tom's and Tom just said how she looked after him after Michael left, took him and ended up staying over because it was late. Normally Tom would be the first to tell Michael of his exploits so Michael gave Tom the benefit of the doubt and believed his story, even though he still had his suspicions.

Just stepping into the pub made Toms stomach turn and he puffed his cheeks, returning to the place where he assaulted his liver in such short time. It was before opening time, the only people already inside were Holly, behind the bar in a black tank top and shirt ready to open up for the day, aligning glasses obsessively to counteract her nerves. She smiled when she saw Tom but felt flat when all he did was greet her friendlily before passing by the bar towards the table where Adam, Simon and Kneecap were sitting.

Michael went over to Holly to make sure she was ready; the plan was for the rest of the lads to be sat in the corner patiently with drinks, while the detective and Holly spoke. Once Holly confronted him with the evidence, the boys would be on hand for any potential fallout.

Michael tugged at Holly's cheek gently, told her to be brave, and wished her luck as he went and quietly joined the others sat in the far corner. While they waited Adam took great pride in recalling the bar they went to up in Leeds where Simon was accosted by an unconvincing transvestite named Christie.

"You never want to be chatted up by someone who has better stubble than you." Adam said to a quiet chorus of laughs, Simon's face went as red as his hair but he took the anecdote with good humour joining in with the mouse like laughter. Holly waited patiently behind the bar right in the middle so when the Detective entered she would be the first thing he saw. Although patient, the nerves were still there, she had become such a strong, confident woman over the last few months but today she did not want to be strong. She gripped one of the lager pumps so hard her fingers were turning white, and out of sight, her left foot was tapping away like a nervous twitch.

The sounds of the metal doors opened at the far end of the pub as the figure of Detective Foreman took centre stage, the brightness of outside shined on him like a spotlight, and sure enough the first thing he saw in his shiny grey suit was the smiling face of Holly. He thought she looked a lot plainer than the other night but he still found her highly enticing. He returned the smile and started over towards her. As is a detective's prerogative, he was observant in his surroundings and when he reached the bar, it did not take him long to spot the five gentlemen sat in the corner nursing their drinks. After greeting Holly with a kiss on the cheek, he curiously said.

"They are in here early" pointing as the table with his forehead, that was when he realised that he knew one of them, he turned ninety degrees to his left and acknowledged the familiar face. "Good morning Mr. Patel." It was a greeting spoken with a chill, adding intimidating intentions to his otherwise sharp tone. Holly leaned over the bar and grabbed one of Foreland's paws getting back his attention.

"Don't you worry about them, they are on a jolly boys outing so they are starting here early, and anyway I thought it was me you came to see?" The detective stopped eyeballing the table of men and leaned his elbows on the bar so his head was level with Holly's.

"That's true," he answered. "I wasn't expecting you to want to see me the very next day; I must have really tempted you. I take it you liked what you got?"

"I did." Holly's answer should have been music to the detective's ears but something sounded wrong, her reply was much too stern, worse so when she repeated herself "I did!" He knew something was amiss; Holly grabbed her phone from the side of the till and showed the detective the same picture he sent last night.

"This is highly illegal detective." Holly said, now Foreman was worried and tried leaning over the bar to grab the phone but Holly stepped back, his face turned to thunder and he looked like he was about to climb over the bar after her but was stopped by a hand clenching his shoulder. It was Tom coming to Holly's rescue like she always knew he would, he had to stretch just to reach Forelands boulder of a shoulder but it was enough of a distraction. His free hand contained his own phone displaying the detective in all his glory. Foreland froze damning his stupidity for letting himself make such a stupid mistake.

"I like it a lot to." Tom said, with his grandfather's cockney heritage encroaching on his voice, trying to sound like an old east end gangster. Although Tom was a hell of a lot smaller than the detective he was confident enough in his scrapping abilities to put up a fight if need be and Foreland could see that in his eyes, Foreland also knew violence now would only make whatever this situation is worse, so he swallowed his pride.

"What is going on here?" He said looking back at Holly, then at Kneecap, suddenly the pieces were starting to connect.

"Unfortunately for us" Tom answered instead of Holly, surprising even himself with how intimidating he sounded. "You stumbled across our little business venture, and unfortunately for you, we had to come up with a way to stop you from pursuing us."

"So you're the one in business with Mr. Patel over there?" The detective said looking Tom up and down with disgust and surprise that someone like him could be running a six-figure pound operation.

"Mr. Kneecap is a valuable member of my team, along with Adam and Simon there?" Adam looked buoyed in the background at getting a shout out and put his thumbs up until Kneecap pulled it down. "But it's me, my friend Michael there and Holly that run the whole thing."

"YOU?" Foreland shouted turning his head like a bullet at Holly. "You're actually involved? A second ago I just assumed you were helping your friends out but now… actually it makes sense, they would need someone strong and smart like you." Almost defeated the Detective turned on the spot looking around at everyone and asked "So what now?"

Michael rose from his chair and stood by Tom's side in solidarity and it was he who answered the detective's question.

"Well I suggest that you leave us alone, unless of course you want your career and family life ruined. I'm sure your colleagues would love to find out how a senior detective has broken the same laws he tries to uphold." Michael had never felt so in control of a situation, he could be forgiven for feeling a bit smug. "And if you don't leave us be, then we have hundreds of copies of your ahem, erotic entertainment ready to be sent to the authorities."

Adam, Simon and Kneecap were now standing just behind Tom and Michael showing allegiance to their bosses. The detective stared down at all of them with a scowl, his normal cool demeanour knocked away from him; he looked over at Holly with a venomous glance then back to face the boys. He straightened his tie and stood tall trying to regain an ounce of dignity.

"That sounds like a fair deal" he conceded, trying his hardest to sound as cocky and as in control as he normally does. "I've got a train to catch." Then without making eye contact with anyone else, he walked through the metal doors of the pub not to be seen again. The slam of the doors closing behind him may as well have been wedding bells for those in the pub as they roared in celebration, each took it in turns to hug, shake hands and generally prance about. Holly anticipated a cuddle from Tom but when he got round to her he simply patted her on the back.

"Holly don't come out from behind the bar just yet; need you to open a bottle of champagne." Michael yelled over the top of the roaring victory chants and Holly smiled in agreement. She popped the cork to a round of cheers from the men. Once the six glasses were full Michael raised a toast "To pornhibition, and long may we prosper." This was met by everyone repeating him and raising their respective glasses in the air. Tom took a sip of his, the thought of alcohol reminded him of his hangover and suddenly with all of the excitement over it returned, he excused himself and much to the disappointment of the party left, once outside and starting on his walk home, he rang Chloe.

"How does Chicken, a box set, my bed and my Queensmouth shirt sound to you right now?" The smile on his face gave away Chloe's answer. "Perfect" he carried on "I'll call for you on the way back."

EPILOGUE

Four days had passed since the confrontation of the detective and with no come back or backlash Holly finally admitted to herself that the coast was probably clear. Holly had the rare opportunity of a Saturday night off and she sat with a couple of girlfriends laughing and gossiping with their vodka and cokes, the problem however was that Holly's attention was divided. Michael, Tom, Adam and Simon were all in the pub that night, all jovial and enjoying what they were doing. Even Kneecap was out doing something that made him happy; he had got himself a private gig as a photographer for a wedding. Holly was worried that she was the only one not happy.

She half-heartedly tried to focus on the conversation with her friends making sure she laughed at the right moments and chipping in the odd remark when she was listening. The conversation soon turned to gossip amongst the patrons of the pub. One of Holly's friends Katie, a caramel toned beauty with jet black hair, pointed her head in the direction of the far end of the bar.

"When did that happen?" She asked judgementally, she was staring at Tom who was sat on a barstool resting comfortably with a glass of fruit juice in front of him. It was not the fact he had a soft drink that irked her interest, it was his company. Opposite the divide of the bar was Chloe looking besotted at Tom's blue eyes. She could not keep her hands off his own, gently stroking them. Neither Holly nor her girlfriends could hear what they were talking about but Holly felt sick, not at how happy Tom looked, but that it was not her making him happy. Tom's smile grew whenever Chloe's did and they made the bar glow. Katie added another observation.

"Maybe he will leave you alone now Hol" She nudged Holly teasing her not aware of her friend's feelings for the man, Holly coming back from a trance looked at Katie saving face.

"Oh yeah, lucky escape aye" Holly said with the fakest of smiles but her two friends did not realise the pretence and laughed with her. Holly insisted they needed somewhere livelier and once she started to sink her drink her friends followed suit and they all left together to take the walk down to the seafront. Holly looked back one last time at Tom and Chloe wondering what could have been before being dragged out of the big metal doors by her friends.

Tom could not help but smile since his rendezvous with Chloe less than a week ago. They had so far, not got bored of each other's constant company and both admitted they had never laughed so much. They could chat about everything and nothing for hours, their views on the wold were similar and conversations could go off on such a tangent that sometimes neither of them could remember what their initial starting point was.

He originally came down the pub in the afternoon to conduct business as usual, and as was the Saturday ritual, he stayed to have a few drinks with the lads. Until Chloe started her shift in the early evening, then Tom abandoned the group to go sit at the bar, even deciding he did not want to drink alcohol, choosing instead to get drunk off Chloe's personality. He told her that, as well as saying he did not want to wake up to her with a hangover, this was sweet coming from Tom and Chloe noticed it.

"Where did this soppy bastard come from?" She said leaning over the bar to play with his hair.

"I honestly don't know," They both laughed. Michael was overlooking and suggested to Adam and Simon that maybe Tom was trying too hard to prove that he could like someone else other than Holly on a level that was above just sex, yet when he saw how fixated each other was on the other he could not deny they made a good match and Tom looked gleeful.

"Well there is no need for it Tom, just be yourself, that's what I like." Chloe consoled her new lover.

"I am being myself, this is apparently what you bring out of me, I didn't know this Tom existed." He sat enjoying his hair being played with "on a serious note though, we will need a chat."

"What's wrong now?" Chloe asked worried about where this could be heading.

"Well, you do know what I do don't you?" Tom looked straight into her eyes, this time more serious than loving, he was aware that Chloe found out along the way the past few months what his new career was. "I don't want you to get caught up in it."

"Of course I know Thomas! You are the biggest porn dealer in the south of England, you are respected, dangerous, good looking, loyal and providing a service that people all over the place want, my boyfriend has all of that, why wouldn't I want to be caught up in it?" Chloe sold Tom well but it was the first time either of them had acknowledged each other as boyfriend or girlfriend, she stepped back ashamed.

"Your boyfriend? I like the sound of that." Tom's response made sure Chloe's happy, bouncy persona returned and stretched over the bar to kiss Tom but he met her half way, neither cared that they were the gossip of the pub and they enjoyed the moment.

"Makes me sick" said Simon as he sat with Michael around a small table in the corner of the pub. Adams drink was also there but he had been coerced into playing pool with another regular. "First you get lucky with some Russian sort last night and now Tom gets the pretty barmaid, where's my happy ending?" Michael couldn't help but look smug much to Simon's annoyance, just minutes before Tom and Chloe's performance at the bar Michael had just relayed his encounter from the previous night to Adam and Simon.

He went out clubbing on a Friday, which had been the norm since he split form Tara, and found himself talking to a twenty-four-year-old Russian, she spoke broken English but enough to get by and converse with Michael. He used his old History lessons about the cold war to find common ground with the blonde, white toothed, short eastern European in her sparkly white dress. Thankfully, she found his bumbling attempts at trying to indulge in Russian culture funny and told him as much. The accent turned Michael on.

Before long, they were back at her hotel room. Michael, feeling a little tipsy, had put on a British sitcom on the satellite box promising to show this Russian student named Tashia more of the British humour he assumed she liked. He slid into bed next to her giggling away with the canned laughter from the sitcom, they then shared a joint, something Michael did not indulge in often and he let the relaxation overcome him. Tashia did not laugh once at the TV show and was confused as to what Michael's intentions were, baffled she asked.

"When we have sex?" Michael was taken aback; he had been out of the game for so long he wasn't sure when to make the move. What he did know however was that he didn't need prompting twice and rolled over on top of the Ravishing woman, it had been a while so he was finished as early as losing at the first shot at Russian roulette. Neither seemed to care however and the next round lasted a bit longer but Michael and Tashia did not go the distance and in the early hours of the morning they pleasantly said goodbyes and Michael headed back to his parents.

So Michael had every reason to feel like a king sat on a throne this evening, it was exactly what he needed since becoming single and was not going to apologise to Simon for boasting, even basking in the fact that he left his underwear behind. Whilst chatting to Simon his phone started ringing. It was from Tara and his emotions changed from being overjoyed; they had not spoken since she returned to university and now Michael felt like he was suffocating, only she would ring now, the day after getting his end away. Guilt tingled in his heart yet he would not show this physically. He almost answered before settling on putting his phone in his trouser pocket, smiling and consoling a jealous Simon. Once the phone was in the pocket, the guilt suddenly disappeared. That was the moment he realised that he was now a different person, he was a gangster, he was rich, he was respected, he was happy.

Printed in Poland
by Amazon Fulfillment
Poland Sp. z o.o., Wrocław

62760924R00073